A King Production presents…

Rich or *Famous*

Rich Because You Can Buy Fame

A Novel

JOY DEJA KING

ISBN 13: 9781942217701
ISBN 10: 1-942217-70-6
Cover concept by Joy Deja King & www.MarionDesigns.com
Cover layout and graphic design by www.MarionDesigns.com
Cover Model: Joy Deja King
Typesetting: Keith Saunders
Editors: Suzy McGlown, Linda Williams

Library of Congress Cataloging-in-Publication Data;
King, Deja Joy
Rich or Famous...Rich Because You Can Buy Fame: a novel/by Joy Deja King
For complete Library of Congress Copyright info visit;
www.joydejaking.com

A King Production
P.O. Box 912, Collierville, TN 38027

A King Production and the above portrayal log are trademarks of A King Production LLC

This Book is Dedicated To My:

Family, Readers and Supporters.
I LOVE you guys so much. Please believe that!!

Rich Because You Can Buy Fame

Lorenzo

Welcome To My World

* ⭐ *

Before I die, if you don't remember anything else I ever taught you, know this. A man will be judged, not on what he has but how much of it. So you find a way to make money and when you think you've made enough, make some more, because you'll need it to survive in this cruel world. Money will be the only thing to save you. As I sat across from Darnell those words my father said to me on his deathbed played in my head.

"Yo, Lorenzo, are you listening to me, did you hear anything I said?"

"I heard everything you said. The problem for you is I don't give a fuck." I responded, giving a casual shoulder shrug as I rested my thumb under my chin with my index finger above my mouth.

"What you mean, you don't give a fuck? We been doing business for over three years now and that's the best you got for me?"

"Here's the thing, Darnell, I got informants all over these streets. As a matter of fact that broad you've had in your back pocket for the last few weeks is one of them."

"I don't understand what you saying," Darnell said swallowing hard. He tried to keep the tone of his voice calm, but his body composure was speaking something different.

"Alexus, has earned every dollar I've paid her to fuck wit' yo' blood suckin' ass. You a fake fuck wit' no fangs. You wanna play wit' my 100 g's like you at the casino. That's a real dummy move, Darnell." I could see the sweat beads gathering, resting in the creases of Darnell's forehead.

"Lorenzo, man, I don't know what that bitch told you but none of it is true! I swear 'bout four niggas ran up in my crib last night and took all my shit. Now that I think about it, that trifling ho Alexus probably had me set up! She fucked us both over!"

I shook my head for a few seconds not believing this muthafucker was saying that shit with a straight face. "I thought you said it was two niggas that ran up in your crib now that shit done doubled. Next thing you gon' spit is that all of Marcy projects was in on the stickup."

"Man, I can get your money. I can have it to you first thing tomorrow. I swear!"

"The thing is I need my money right now." I casually stood up from my seat and walked towards Darnell who now looked like he had been dipped in water. Watching him fall apart in front of my eyes made up for the fact that I would never get back a dime of the money he owed me.

"Zo, you so paid, this shit ain't gon' even faze you. All I'm asking for is less than twenty-four hours. You can at least give me that," Darnell pleaded.

"See, that's your first mistake, counting my pockets. My money is *my* money, so yes this shit do faze me."

"I didn't mean it like that. I wasn't tryna disrespect you. By this time tomorrow you will have your money and we can put this shit behind us." Darnell's eyes darted around in every direction instead of looking directly at me. A good liar, he was not.

"Since you were robbed of the money you owe me and the rest of my drugs, how you gon' get me my dough? I mean the way you tell it, they didn't leave you wit' nothin' but yo' dirty draws."

"I'll work it out. Don't even stress yourself, I got you, man."

"What you saying is that the nigga you so called aligned yourself with, by using my money and my product, is going to hand it back over to you?"

"Zo, what you talking 'bout? I ain't aligned myself wit' nobody. That slaw ass bitch Alexus feeding you lies."

"No, that's you feeding me lies. Why don't you admit you no longer wanted to work for me? You felt you was big shit and could be your own boss. So you used my money and product to buy your way in with this other nigga to step in my territory. But you ain't no boss you a poser. And your need to perpetrate a fraud is going to cost you your life."

"Lorenzo, don't do this man! This is all a big misunderstanding. I swear on my daughter I will have your money tomorrow. Fuck, if you let me leave right now I'll have that shit to you tonight!" I listened to Darnell stutter his words.

My men, who had been patiently waiting in each corner of the warehouse, dressed in all black, loaded with nothing but artillery, stepped out of the darkness ready to obliterate the enemy I had once considered my best worker. Darnell's eyes widened as he witnessed the men who had saved and protected him on numerous occasions, as he dealt with the vultures he encountered in the street life, now ready to end his.

"Don't do this, Zo! Pleeease," Darnell was now on his knees begging.

"Damn, nigga, you already a thief and a backstabber. Don't add, going out crying like a bitch to that too. Man the fuck up. At least take this bullet like a soldier."

"I'm sorry, Zo. Please don't do this. I gotta daughter that need me. Pleeease man, I'll do anything. Just don't kill me." The tears were pouring down Darnell's face and instead of softening me up it just made me even more pissed at his punk ass.

"Save your fuckin' tears. You shoulda thought about your daughter before you stole from me. You're the worse sort of thief. I invite you into my home, I make you a part of my family and you steal from me, you plot against me. Your daughter doesn't need you. You have nothing to teach her."

My men each pulled out their gat ready to attack and I put my hand up motioning them to stop. For the first time since Darnell arrived, a calm gaze spread across his face.

"I knew you didn't have the heart to let them kill me, Zo. We've been through so much together. I mean you Tania's God Father. We bigger than this and we will get through it," Darnell said, halfway smiling as he began getting off his knees and standing up.

"You're right, I don't have the heart to let them kill you, I'ma do that shit myself." Darnell didn't even have a chance to let what I said resonate with him because I just sprayed that muthafucker like the piece of shit he was. "Clean this shit up," I said, stepping over Darnell's bullet ridden body as I made my exit.

Dior

American Dream

* ⋆*⋆*⋆ *

I watched through the window as the helicopter descended upon the center of the 25 story marble-clad hotel roof's landing pad. The bright lights lit up the city that never sleeps. I remained in the helicopter until all blades had stopped spinning and the ground handler opened my door.

A brisk New York City chill greeted me as I stepped out the helicopter. I quickly wrapped my full length chinchilla around my body, yearning for instant warmth. "Follow me, Mr. Stone is waiting for you," the handler said taking my hand. I walked swiftly but with caution not wanting my five inch pencil thin heel to get caught in a crack and scratched in the slightest.

We took the private elevator down and the doors opened up to at least a 6,000-square foot room laced out in walls of partitioned glass, marble floors and a grand piano that had a 22-gold carat chandelier above it. I knew that because earlier, when Sway called me in one of his coke induced highs, he kept going on and on about how hard his dick was watching some naked girl dance on top of the piano. But he wanted to make it clear, that his dick wasn't hard because of the naked girl, it was because he imagined the 22-gold carat chandelier crashing down on top of her and her body breaking up into small pieces of crystal, then spreading down the piano and turning into quicksand—then everyone in the room is drowning in the quicksand, except for him of course because he always survives everything. That was the illogical yet creative way his mind worked. But the craziness of Sway Stone is what many said was the root of his success. Nobody could deny Sway was a superstar and one of the biggest hip hop icons of his time.

"My muse is finally here," Sway declared before sticking his tongue down my throat. I tolerated his wet and sloppy kiss and even pretended to enjoy it. "Take off your coat," he demanded. "I want to see how you look in the dress I picked out for you."

I let the chinchilla fall to the floor revealing the cutout metallic feather and vintage cocktail mini paired with sparkling silver heels. Sway twirled me around as if I was his own personal dress up Barbie with an approving grin. "I knew this dress would be blazin' on you. This shit is perfect! And later when we fuck I want you to keep it on. Don't take *anything* off," he stressed. I stood staring into Sway's deep brown eyes wondering if he was always so self absorbed or did the fame do it to him.

"Dior, did you hear what the fuck I said?" he barked, switching gears in a matter of seconds. His calm even tenor had now turned rough and thunderous. This was typical behavior when Sway didn't feel you were giving him your full attention. He expected responses to come as quick as they popped in his head. I learned that early in our relationship but I had a slight slip which I knew how to recover from.

"Yes, baby, I heard you," I said caressing the side of his face. "I promise I won't take anything off."

"Well don't take so long to speak up next time," he said as he cupped the bottom of my ass and pulled me closer, once again doing the deep throat with his tongue. All was forgotten for now until of course I slipped up again which was inevitable.

Sway gripped my hand and led me to the long suede couch that had an orgasmic view of the city and Hudson River. "What's up Dior," Lori, one of his many fake hangers-on's smiled and said.

I knew for a fact she had been sucking his dick

for the last year and couldn't stand me because I was Sway's current main chick and was outlasting all his previous tricks. I couldn't stand her either but for a different reason. See, instead of just going about her business after her two week fuck fest ended with Sway, she decided to become a constant fixture in his inner circle by being the on-call whore for him and all his boys.

That shit annoyed the hell out of me. I believe in every chick doing what the fuck they have to do to stay relevant in the game because trust, I have gotten down and will get down for mine but her behavior was the definition of a basic bitch. But the longer I ran around in the 'industry cliques' it became clear that basic bitches were the majority. Every rapper, singer, athlete and pseudo celebrities kept a gang of basic bitches around them. Now I had done a lot of shit to get to where I was at this very moment but I was never nobody's basic bitch.

"Lori, why do you always speak to me when you know I can't stand you?" The handful of people that were standing around the couch including Lori all looked at me with a blank stare. I asked the question in such a non-threatening tone they didn't know how to take it.

"My baby has such a sick sense of humor. I love it!" Sway grinned as he kissed my neck. His reaction thawed out the cold chill and everybody laughed as if I had been joking by what I said. Of course it was true and deep down Lori knew it. But what could she do because for now I was the head bitch in charge.

"Lori, I left my fur on the floor. Go pick it up for me please. Thanks." I turned to Sway and glided my hand up and down his inner thigh.

"You're making my dick so hard," Sway grabbed the nape of my neck, pulling me close and continued whispering in my ear, "I wanna fuck you, right here on this couch in front of everybody."

"Go 'head, there's nothing stopping you." Sway slid his hand inside the top of my dress and let his fingers slither across my nipple. He played with it for a few minutes as he went from kissing me to staring in my eyes.

"You're crazier than me."

"You just now figured that out."

"You would really let me fuck you right here?"

"I'm down for whatever. I'm sure everybody in this room has fucked before so we wouldn't be showing them nothing they ain't already seen."

"Yo, Sway, come here."

"Can't you see I'm fuckin' busy."

"Gee on the phone. He need to speak with you 'bout the show tomorrow."

"What about it?"

"There's been a few changes and he need to discuss it wit' you." Sway let out a deep sigh, obviously irritated that his sex fantasy was being interrupted. But Gee was his manager and as fucked up as Sway was, when it came to business he always handled his.

"Dior, stay right here. I'll be right back."

"No problem, baby, I'm not going anywhere." As I watched Sway walk away I noticed that my fur was still on the floor. I turned around and Lori was looking at me frowned up. "Is there a reason you haven't picked up my fur?"

"Yeah, because I don't work for you," Lori spit running her fingers through her cropped red hair.

"You work for Sway so you work for me."

"I don't work for Sway."

"Oh, so you do all that fucking and sucking for fun it's not a job?"

"I'm just doing what you do, Dior."

"Oh babygirl, that's where you got it wrong. I do work for Sway but unlike you I'm compensated for my services. That's why I'm wearing a chinchilla and you're going to be picking it up."

"I ain't picking up shit!"

"Yes you are because if you don't I'll tell Sway how disrespectful you are and to toss your whorish ass out of here. And trust me, he will do it because right now I'm holding his balls you're just licking them when I'm unavailable."

"You're a complete bitch!"

"So true, but that's beside the point."

"You might be on top now but you will fall. I just hope I'm around to witness it."

"You either shut the fuck up and get my fur or your days of parading around industry parties on Sway's tip are over."

"Baby, I'm back and I brought you a present," Sway said, before handing me a small vile of coke. I looked up at him and didn't say anything. "Is everything okay?" he asked moving a loose curl from over my eye.

"I'm just waiting for Lori to do something I asked."

"What's the hold up?" Sway questioned Lori shrugging his shoulders.

"No hold up. I'm taking care of it right now."

I simply smiled and took the vile of coke from Sway. I opened it and put it down on the black marble table. I reached for a card from a deck of playing cards and made two neat little lines. I took the rolled up hundred Sway had in his hand and then held one nostril closed with my finger. I made sure to keep my mouth closed to keep from blowing on the other line. I put the hundred into my open nostril and sucked in while chasing the line. When I was done I inhaled sharply for a few times. I immediately repeated it all over again for the second line using my other nostril.

As I sat back, relaxed and let the drug take hold, two things crossed my mind. First, I thought about how in around twenty minutes backdrip would start flowing from my nasal cavity down my throat. It was a mixture of snot and coke and the taste was revolting. That's why if possible I would make sure to have a strongly flavored drink handy so the taste wouldn't be so disgusting.

After thinking about that for a few minutes my mind switched to how the life I was living was so different from what most considered being the norm. I always heard people talking about reaching the American Dream: Married, 2.5 kids, dog, nice house with a white picket fence and a great family vacation once a year. I still didn't understand what the hell 2.5 kids meant and honestly I could care less. It was like when I would go to sleep at night, the only dream I ever had was to be famous. I imagined being draped in designer clothes, just like the ones I was wearing tonight, walking red carpets, being in the spotlight and every girl in the world wishing they could walk in my shoes. Yes, that was my American dream and even in my coke induced high I knew I would do anything to make that dream a reality.

Lorenzo

How Life Changes

✦✶✯✶✦

"I can't believe he's dead! No he can't be, he can't be dead...he can't be dead!" I listened to Darnell's baby mother scream that out for about fifteen minutes. I was trying to be patient because I understood that she was mourning the loss of a man she loved who was also the father of her child. But I knew the nigga didn't deserve not one of her tears which made the task of me seeming to care about his death a difficult one.

"Lala, calm down, it'll be okay." I held her closely trying to console her as much as possible.

"Mommy, mommy, why are you crying? Who

is dead?" I looked up and saw Tania running down the stairs. She was such a beautiful little girl and luckily it all came from her mother and she didn't resemble her father at all. I might not have been able to stand the child if she had. "Uncle Lorenzo, why is my mommy crying?"

"Your mother is going through a hard time right now but she'll pull through," I said, trying to reassure her the best I could.

"Tania, go back upstairs with grandma," Lala managed to say through uncontrollable sobs.

"But I want to stay with you." Tania was now holding on to her mother's leg and I had flashbacks to when I was a little boy and I begged my mother not to leave my father and me. She had one piece of luggage as she stood at the front door. I held her leg so tightly and tears wouldn't stop pouring from my eyes. But as hard as I cried and as much as I begged my mother still walked out the door. After that I promised myself I would never cry over another woman again.

"Tania, listen to your mother and go back upstairs." I bent down so I was eye level with her. "I'll take care of your mother and when we're done she'll come upstairs to get you."

"Did something happen to my daddy because he said he would always take care of us?"

"You don't have to worry about that. I'll always take care of you. Now go upstairs. I'll be up there in a minute." Tania let go of her mother's leg and slowly walked toward the stairs, looking back every couple of steps. I gave her a reassuring smile knowing that as content as I was with her father being dead, she was innocent and didn't deserve to feel the pain she would no doubt endure.

"Lala, you have to pull it together, if not for your own sanity then for your daughter."

"I just don't understand how this could've happened. I saw him last night, Lorenzo and he was fine. How can you hold somebody in your arms one day and the very next day they dead. That shit don't make no sense."

"Lala, you know how this game work. Every time you walk out the door you risking your life."

"You have to find whoever robbed and killed him and make them pay for taking his life, Lorenzo. Darnell held it down for you for years and was always loyal. He deserves for you to seek retribution against the muthafucker that took him from his family."

"I will but let me handle that. I don't want you worrying about what goes on in the streets. All I want you to do is take care of Tania and help her through this. I want you to take this," I said handing Lala a bag of money. "There will be more of this to come."

"Lorenzo, this is too much."

"No it isn't. Tania is my Goddaughter and she'll never want for anything. That, I promise you."

"Thank you. You were always good to us and I know how much Darnell loved you."

"I'ma go upstairs and say bye to Tania. I have to go out of town but when I get back I'll come check on you."

"Lorenzo, thank you again."

"Stop thanking me. This is what family do, take care of each other." I watched as the tears continued to flow down Lala's face and was disgusted. I felt no regret for killing Darnell but I hated that even in death he had to make me feel something. I wanted to never have to see Lala or Tania's face again so I wouldn't be reminded of Darnell's punk ass but I believed in taking care of my people. And whether I liked it or not the day I accepted being Tania's God father we became family.

I kissed Lala on her forehead and went upstairs to say goodbye to Tania. When I reached the hallway I could see Tania sitting on her canopy bed with her grandmother holding her. She was brushing the doll's hair that I gave her last year for her 5th birthday. I remember not even wanting to get the doll. But a chick I was dealing with at the time, told me that kids want more than money thrown at them on their birthday, they like to get a gift. That shit sounded crazy to me because growing up all I wanted was money, it didn't matter the occasion. But when I saw the way Tania's eyes lit up when she ripped up the wrapping paper and saw the doll, I knew shorty was right.

Instead of going into Tania's bedroom I turned around. I went back downstairs and left. Watching her in that moment, I made up my mind that I would never be a God father again and if possible never have children of my own. In the treacherous business I was in, being responsible for an innocent child's emotions was a burden I had no desire to carry.

"How did Lala take it?" Alexus asked me when I got in the car. I was quiet for a second before starting up the Range. I kept my head down because I wasn't in the mood to talk and instantly regretted bringing Alexus with me, even if I left her in the car.

"How the fuck do you think she took it? You ask the dumbest fuckin' questions sometimes."

"Don't bark at me, you the one who fuckin' killed him!" Without a second thought I reached over and wrapped my hands around Alexus's throat.

"Like I said, sometimes you say the dumbest shit. That's twice in less than a minute, you know what happens the third time." I locked eyes with Alexus, holding a steady glare. The fear her face encompassed let me know that she understood I was not playing. "I didn't kill nobody and I better not ever hear that you said that to a soul, living or dead."

Alexus was trying to let me know she wouldn't but my hands were gripping her neck so fucking tight her shit was frozen. Dealing with Lala and seeing Tania had me so on edge I was ready to snap Alexus's neck but knew that was the wrong move. I slowly eased up the pressure from her throat and she immediately started gasping for air like death had been one breath away. While Alexus tried to pull it together, I drove off pissed that in a few hours I had to be on a plane.

"Lorenzo, you could've killed me," Alexus finally managed to say.

"That was the point I wanted to make."

"As far back as we go you could really do that?"

"Yo, you caught me at a bad time. I got a lot of shit on my mind. And I wasn't in the mood for your reckless talk."

"I get it."

"Good, now where am I dropping you off at 'cause I gotta catch this flight."

"Where you going?"

"Miami."

"You can have me do all your dirty work and choke me up but you never take me to the fun shit."

"There ain't nothing fun about this trip, it's business. Honestly, I wish I could send you or somebody else in my place but I have to show my face at this party."

"Yeah, whatever," she said in a low voice. I turned to look in Alexus's direction and she was rubbing her throat as if she was still in disbelief that less than a few minutes ago I had my hands wrapped around it.

Alexus and I shared what most would describe as an intimate relationship but yet we weren't fucking. She had been the closest thing I ever had to a wife without consummating the marriage. But what I had with her was more valuable than pussy— we had trust. I trusted Alexus to carry out shit for me that I wouldn't let anybody else do but I always kept her on the low. Only a handful of people in my circle knew about our relationship, that's why I was able to use her to bring down Darnell. She was my ride or die chick without ever tasting the dick. But like all wives, sometimes she would step out of line and I had to put her back in her place. But then like a good husband I would also have to slow my roll and make her feel appreciated.

"Next time I have to go to Miami, I'll make sure you go to."

"You mean that?"

"You know damn well I don't say shit unless I mean it."

"That ain't nothing but the truth."

"When I go back again for some business, I'll bring you and we can stay a few extra days. You can do a little shopping. Hit the beach and a few parties. You've been working hard, you deserve it."

"Thank you. I didn't think you noticed but it's good to know you do."

"Of course I notice. But you still need to watch that mouth," I said, before turning the music up. I wasn't in the mood for any further conversation and Alexus knew when I turned the music up that meant no more talking.

When I arrived at Dream Nightclub, I immediately wanted to go back to my poolside bungalow at the W. Both were located in the heart of South Beach except in my bungalow I could get some fucking privacy and peace, something that would be impossible to obtain on a Saturday night at a popular club. It was typical for the place to be packed but tonight it was painfully congested. Not only were all the local groupies out in full force, many flew in from different states because tonight they were celebrating Phenomenon's birthday. So of course every thirsty broad from the east to west coast wanted to make sure their presence was felt. They knew the industry heavyweights and other celebrities would be coming through to show the new rap wiz on the block some love. But unlike the other people coming to pop bottles and all that other bullshit, my only intent was handling business. I had invested heavily in Phenomenon's career so my stake in his success was huge. I was what you'd call a silent partner. The millions I was making in my lucrative drug dealings was the key to funding Phenomenon's leap to stardom. Although his people would continuously ask me to play a bigger part in his business dealings, my role was low key, just the way I liked it. But for certain special occasions, like a massive blowout birthday party, I would show my respect to Phenomenon and his team that were doing the hands on work that I wanted no part of.

"You good?" I heard one of Phenomenon's handlers ask as I sat quietly watching everything going on around me.

"I'm straight."

"P wanted you to come over to sit at his booth."

"I'm good for now, but let him know I'll be over there shortly." He nodded his head and headed back over to Phenomenon's table. I glanced around the 2 level club which had three main spots, the Main Room, The Nugget Room and the Candle Room. The club was around 8,500 square feet and had about a 600 person capacity but tonight it felt like it was at least a thousand motherfuckers in the spot. As I continued to size up the area, I noticed complete mayhem breaking out towards the front of the club. My two security dudes that I had with me the majority of the time moved forward to see what the hell was going on. Then it seemed like every bird in the entire club stopped what they were doing and began flocking in the same direction.

"Who the fuck is these broads breaking their neck to see?" I asked Brice who was closest to me.

"It's too many of them. I can't see through the crowd."

I leaned forward and a few seconds later I watched as some nigga with a fucking ridiculous entourage came strolling through the crowd like they owned the spot. I zeroed in on who looked to be the leader of the pack and quickly recognized him as Sway Stone. He and his entire crew had on all black except for the young lady, whose hand he was holding tightly. There was no doubt everybody knew who Sway was but the lady walked with so much confidence and swagger you would've thought she was the international star. She was wearing one of the shortest red dresses I had ever seen with some thigh high black boots. On most women the outfit would've looked whorish but with her body shape and size she was able to pull it off and make it seem sophisticated sexy. I found myself staring at her until she sat down with Sway in a private booth next to Phenomenon. She then pulled out a cigarette, lit it up and began smoking. I absolutely detested a woman who smoked but the way her long slender fingers held on to the cancer stick made it appealing.

I decided to take Phenomenon up on his offer and sit at his booth. As I made my way, I had a security guard in front and one in back of me. As I got closer to the table I turned in the woman's direction and watched as she blew smoke from her glossy full lips. I briefly caught her eye or at least I thought I did but she quickly pushed back a loose curl from over her eye and took a sip of her champagne as if she hadn't noticed me.

"Yo Zo, I'm glad you finally decided to come over and show a brotha some love," Phenomenon said as I sat down.

"I was letting you get settled in before I came crashing your party. There's been women coming at you nonstop and I didn't want to interrupt," I laughed.

"You know I ain't checkin' for none of these chicks like that. One of these hoes will have a nigga fucked up behind some bullshit. I got too much shit poppin' off to let that happen."

"That's true but it's only right you have a little fun too."

"No doubt! You know I'm gettin' it in but I'm careful. What I need is to get me a main shorty that rock wit' me all the time. Like look at that nigga Sway," Phenomenon pointed his chin in their direction. "Did you see the bad bitch he came up in here wit?"

"Nah, I didn't notice," I lied and said.

"Shiiit, I need one of those. I can dress her up, take her everywhere wit' me and not even worry about these other broads. And every now and then when I feel like switching it up, I can."

"You already sounding like a veteran in the game. So all I can say is be careful 'cause you still a rookie."

"Hey Phenomenon..." a teenage looking groupie smiled, cutting off our conversation. I welcomed the interruption because I wanted to focus my attention back on the person who motivated me to come over to sit down with him in the first place. I was trying to size her up without it being obvious. As I caught myself trying to sneak a peek, I couldn't believe this woman had me acting like a nigga with a school boy crush. I didn't have those even when I was a teenager. But I wanted her and I rarely ever wanted anything besides money so I had to have her.

I sat patiently and watched as they were drinking, smoking, dancing and continued this same routine over and over again. I was waiting for a small window of opportunity to make my move and finally it came. Sway and a bunch of others went upstairs and the woman I was checking for stayed in the booth with one other female. They weren't engaging in any conversation so I figured it was the perfect moment to see where her head was at.

"Would you like another bottle of champagne?" I offered noticing her glass was low and there wasn't another bottle on the table.

"Excuse me?" she questioned with a slight northern accent.

"I said would you like another bottle? I noticed your glass was empty."

"Sure," she said nonchalantly. She lifted her glass up and as I poured the champagne she looked off as if trying not to acknowledge me.

"So what's your name?"

"Oh, since you gave me some champagne I'm supposed to tell you my name?"

"You don't have to but I would like if you did." She paused for a few seconds and I could tell she was quickly trying to size me up, something I had been doing to her all night.

"Dior, my name is Dior."

"That name fits you."

"Why is that?"

"It just does. Why don't you let me take you out to dinner, Dior?"

"You must didn't see who I came in here with."

"Why would you think that?"

"Because if you had you would know that I don't do dinner with just anybody."

"I wouldn't expect any less because I'm not just anybody."

"Well you sure ain't Sway Stone and that's who I'm with."

"There ain't nothing Sway Stone can do for you that I can't do."

"Oh really?"

"I didn't stutter."

"Can you have me walking down red carpets? No. Can you have the paparazzi breaking their necks trying to take our pictures? No. Can you have me all up in the blogs and magazines with everybody checking for me because I'm on the arm of a superstar? No. Can you have me in the front row of the hottest designers during fashion week? No. So as cute as you are, you can't do for me everything that Sway can."

"So all you're interested in is being in the limelight?"

"I call it fame, baby. That's what being with Sway is going to get me because I need a lot more than free champagne to make me happy."

I laughed to myself at the lack of shame this woman had in her game. Running the streets I had dealt with all sorts of women but this one right here was a piece of work. She was so blatantly shallow that it made me find her even more intriguing.

"Dior, just go out to dinner with me. I promise you, after doing so you won't want anybody else but me. And trust, Sway has nothing on my pockets."

"I don't care about your money because it can't buy me what I want, which is fame. So thanks for the champagne but I need to go find my man before one of these scavengers in here tries to take my place."

With those parting words, just like that she was gone. In all my years of dealing with women I had never met one that didn't bite and never did I have to play the money card to get them to do so. But here I was justifying my pockets and she still didn't want any part of me. I didn't even know how to classify her. It couldn't be a gold-digger because she didn't want my bread. It couldn't be a ho 'cause she wasn't giving up no pussy. The only thing I could come up with was a fame chaser. But could I really fault her for that? I chased money all day long so we both chased but she was chasing something else. I couldn't help but think that maybe I needed to consider doing the same thing.

Dior

Shut It Down

✦✦★✦✦

I struggled to open my eyes as the sun glared through the massive floor to ceiling length windows. With the tip of my fingers I gently massaged my closed eyelids and slowly worked my way outwards trying to center and calm my mind. Waking up groggy and sluggish was typical so by now I knew what worked and what didn't. Within a few minutes I was able to gain some focus and the first thing I noticed was Sway spread out in the middle of the bed and some chick that was a mutt curled up on the other side of him. I couldn't tell what she was mixed with but with Miami girls most of the time you didn't. I lifted the silk sheet off of me exposing my naked body.

The crazy part was, I didn't even remember taking off my clothes. I headed straight to the kitchen and opened the drawer to get my bottle of Adderral. I didn't even bother getting a glass instead I grabbed the bottle of champagne to wash down my pill.

This was like a routine that I never got tired of. If I needed something to wake me up and keep my adrenaline going all day, Adderral never let me down. It was like being on crack without smoking a pipe. It would even kill my hunger and make me forget to eat. But to keep up with the lifestyle Sway lived I had no choice. He popped pills to get up and some more to get down which didn't include all the other recreational drugs he did, so all I was trying to do was keep up.

"Hey, do you have something I can put on? I'm about to take a shower and my clothes smell like smoke. So of course I don't want to put them back on."

The girls loud bubbly voice almost made me drop my bottle of champagne because I didn't even notice her. She was standing in the living room naked just like me. It took me a moment to respond to her because I zoomed in on a floral vein tattoo that went up the curve of her waist. As long as it was the shit was actually hot.

"I like your tattoo," I said casually and kept drinking from the bottle.

"Thanks," she grinned as if excited I gave her a

compliment. "So what about those clothes because we're about the same size," she said still grinning.

"Oh doll, I don't share my clothes. You'll be leaving here in the same thing you came in—smoke smelling and all."

"I don't understand." It was funny because she was totally giving me the perplexed look.

"I get it. You think because we shared a bed and a man, sharing clothes would be no big deal. Besides the fact that I never share my clothes unless they're last season and I'm done with them for good. I'm never going to see you again so I won't get my clothes back."

"Huh?"

"Huh," I said back mockingly.

"What is with you?"

"The question is what is with you? What are you twelve? What don't you get? You got to fuck Sway. Okay great! When you leave here call all your girlfriends and let them know because it was a onetime thing, trust me. You know how many times I've woken up and he's had a different girl in the bed with him. You're not special sweetie. If he planned on keeping you around you wouldn't be asking me for a change of clothes because they would already be in the closet, like mine. Now if you would excuse me, there's a video shoot we're going to in a couple of hours and I need to take a shower."

"Good morning," Sway said walking out the

bedroom with his dick swinging everywhere as I was ending the conversation.

"Hey baby, I was just about to come get back in the bed with you," the girl said giving a full watt smile.

"What the fuck are you still doing here? You need some cab money or something to get home?"

Of course the girl's smile turned to a straight frown and then she rested her eyes on me. I simply mouthed; *I told you so* and walked to the bedroom. As I went in the bathroom and turned on the shower I could hear the girl damn near begging for Sway to let her stay. Then she was trying to give him her phone number so he could keep in touch with her. It was the same song and dance I had witnessed on too many occasions to count and every time each chick made the same mistake. They would throw the pussy at him and then sniff after him like a lost puppy.

As the hot water drenched my body I thought about when I met Sway. Like the rest of these broads, I gave him the pussy too in a blink of an eye but the difference was he had to come looking for me. I made sure after I fucked him every which way I could that when he woke up I was gone. That shit was planned and strategized the same way Hollywood actresses plot to get the leading role in a movie.

The guy that invited and introduced me to Sway, at his party was his stylist, so I knew that he would have a way of getting in touch with me. Sure enough that morning he woke up and I was gone he called me. It was from a blocked number and I never accept blocked calls so he left me a message with his phone number. I didn't even return the call. I couldn't help but laugh out loud thinking back to how everything went down. Then the next day his stylist called me letting me know that Sway was trying to get in touch with me. I played it off like I hadn't checked my messages. He then gave me the number himself and told me to call Sway when we got off the phone, of course I didn't.

My girl Brittani who attended all the industry events had already told me that in a few days Sway's manager was having a birthday party. So I went there looking like a fucking billion dollars. Every dude's tongue in there was wagging. And when I strutted my ass pass Sway's table like I didn't even notice him he grabbed my arm and never let it go. He grilled me on why I hadn't returned his phone call. I acted like I had been so busy that it slipped my mind. He was dumbstruck and kept me in his back and front pocket from that night on, which was cool with me.

From the second I decided to go after Sway I knew I would never lock him down and it wasn't my intention. It was no secret he was a whore and he loved living the life of being rich and famous. That was the main reason I made him a target.

Some superstars hid from the spotlight but Sway welcomed it and that was the type of man I needed if I was going to get my shine. It seemed like overnight I was in all the magazines and popular blogs. At first they referenced me as his 'gal pal' but once it became apparent I wasn't a onetime on the scene chick it didn't take long for the media to address me by one name, 'Dior'.

"What's up, Sway! I feel honored that you came through to bless my video," the hottest new rapper on the rise, Phenomenon said to Sway when we arrived.

"I got you! Your lyrics are crazy and this joint is bananas. You gon' kill the charts wit' this. You goin' straight to the top, watch!"

"That's my goal and with the budget the label is giving me for this video, that's what they hoping too." Both of them laughed and did some more small talk before Phenomenon went back on set. I knew we would be here for awhile because that's how it went on a video shoot. I had been on several especially since I started dating Sway. The shit was redundant but I just considered it as part of the job.

As Sway and I got comfortable in the private area they had set up for him I could hear the video director screaming and he wouldn't stop.

"What the fuck is going on over there?" Sway asked out loud walking towards the open area by the set. They had a bedroom scene laid out and the director had now lowered his voice but you could see the anger on his face. He was talking to a young looking guy who I figured was an assistant or intern. As we walked up closer we could hear what the director was saying.

"Tell that girl to get her ass out here right now. We don't have all fuckin' day to wait on her!" The guy immediately ran to the dressing room and knocked on the door. I saw the door slightly open and he was talking to who I assumed was the girl although I couldn't see her face. Then the door closed and the guy came walking back towards the director with a look of gloom plastered across his face.

"She won't come out," the guy said in a defeated tone.

"You didn't say what I think you just said?"

"She doesn't feel..."

"I don't give a fuck what she feels!" The director barked, cutting the guy off. "She isn't getting paid to feel shit but what I tell her to." In the midst of their dialogue I saw the dressing room door open and the girl came out with a bathrobe on. As she got nearer her eyes seemed slightly red as if she had been crying.

"I apologize for making you wait." She sounded

sincere and had a sweet, innocent look. Not typical of chicks I had seen on previous video sets.

"Whatever, just take off your robe so we can shoot this scene. We've already wasted enough time," the director said coldly.

"I don't want to take off my robe."

"If you want to wait until you get in the bed, that's fine, just get over there."

"I mean, I don't want to take my robe off at all. When my agent told me about this job she didn't mention that I had to be in some skimpy bra and panties."

"What the fuck did you think you were gonna wear? This is a fuckin' hip hop video not a damn PTA meeting!"

"I understand that, but this is my first video shoot and..."

"And it will be your last if you don't take off that fuckin' robe and get in the bed." The director could see the resistance on the girl's face so he wouldn't let up. "Do you know how many women wanted the lead role for this video? We had supermodels, top notch actresses and every video model you can think of trying to get this part. But Phenomenon and his label wanted an unknown so I made the stupid mistake of picking you."

"I'm sorry. I do want this part and I can do everything else but I don't want to be on television in front of millions of people practically naked."

I listened and stared at the girl and for some reason I actually felt sorry for her, which was a rarity for me. Sympathy wasn't an emotion that was easy for me to come by. Honestly I thought she was a fool for not snatching this opportunity and holding it tight. The way the music industry was now, very few artists had videos that were highly anticipated but this was definitely one of them. When the director told the girl about all the women that were vying for the lead, he wasn't exaggerating. The exposure alone would make them hot for a second and if they played their cards right it would buy them a few more minutes. If parading around in your bra and panties would get you that I didn't understand what the big fuckin' deal was. It wasn't like she was getting butt ass naked and making a sex video with a pseudo singer.

"I'ma ask you one last time to take off your robe and go get in the bed," the director said calmly. "If you're not gonna do it, then get the fuck off my set," he bolted, leaving a deafening sound in all our ears. The girl burst out in tears and ran off the set. I was tempted to go after her but what would I say. *You're making a fuckin' mistake, choke it up, take off the robe and get the shit over with*. But I didn't because it was clear she wasn't cut out for this.

"I can't believe this shit! This is what the fuck I get for using an amateur," the director yelled out to anybody that would listen. "I'll never be able to wrap this shoot up today if I don't find somebody asap! Who the fuck am I gonna find to do this shit at the last minute?"

"I'll do it," I said raising my hand and stepping forward like a student would volunteer and do in junior high when trying to score brownie points with the teacher. The director turned and looked in my direction, noticing me for the first time. Luckily when I'm by Sway's side he always has me in fighting form so my appearance was on point. I had on a one piece gray short jumper with a black leather belt that clinched tightly on my waist. It highlighted all my best assets without making me look desperate and cheap.

"The job is yours," he said with a look of surprise that he had a female right under his nose that fit the bill.

"No the fuck it's not!" Sway stepped forward and said just as quickly.

"Sway, what's the dilemma? She's perfect." The director clearly didn't want to cause a problem with Sway but at the same time wanted to convince him it should be a go.

"Yeah, she's perfect for me, not for your video."

"Man, I'm pressed for time. If I'm not able to use her then I'll have to wait and finish this video tomorrow which will put me way over budget. I just want to borrow her for a little while, I promise to give her right back," he said in a joking way, trying to break the wall Sway had put up but Sway wasn't budging.

"Then I guess you shit out of luck if you gambling on me letting you use her, 'cause it ain't happenin.'"

"Baby, it's just a video. You should let me do it."

"Yo, shut the fuck up and go sit yo' ass down! I can't believe you volunteered for this shit in the first place!"

"Whatever you say, baby."

"You fuckin' right! And don't forget that shit!" I walked off the set and sat down pissed like a mutherfucka. That was the one major obstacle I had dealing with Sway—the only gig I was supposed to have was pleasing him. Once I became his permanent arm candy, people were constantly coming at him for me to do magazine spreads, interviews just anything to know who was this chick that had been able to hold Sway's attention, but he would always shut it down. The chance I had today was too fucking good to pass up. I figured since I volunteered in front of everybody Sway would go ahead and let me do it so he didn't appear petty but he still shut the shit down. He was once again blocking my chance of getting closer to having my own fame outside of him.

"Don't you ever do no shit like that again or I'll fuck you up," he threatened, interrupting my own cursing out I was giving him in my head.

"Baby, I was just trying to help. The director was in a bind. I didn't think you would mind."

"I don't keep you around for you to think. I do all the thinking for you. So unless I tell you to do something, don't volunteer to do shit."

"It won't happen again."

"It better not, now let's go."

"But you didn't shoot your guest spot yet."

"Fuck this video! I ain't doin' no fuckin' guest spot." I didn't say a word. When Sway got in one of his funks it was best to remain quiet and follow his lead. His bodyguards rushed us out to the awaiting car and I knew for the rest of the night I would have to deal with him snorting coke and poppin' shit.

Lorenzo

I Can Make You A Star

★ ⭐ ★

I watched as Dior made her exit with Sway and by no means was she happy but she was playing her position true to form. I watched from a distance as everything played out and I had to admit I found it amusing, especially after the conversation I had with her last night. Dior was positive that being with Sway would garner her all the fame she craved but instead that nigga was blocking harder than an NFL offensive guard.

"Yo, did you see that nigga Sway bounce! I can't believe he broke out like that." Phenomenon was shaking his head in disappointment. I knew he admired that cat but I was too busy laughing at Dior in my mind that I wasn't really paying him attention like I should have.

"Son, you good," was all I could muster.

"Whatever. I guess that egotistical bullshit people be saying he on is really true. And on the real, his girl would've been perfect for the video. Now we gotta scramble to find somebody else on some last minute shit. This would've been a good look for everybody. So not only is he causing me to go over budget on my first major video but he ain't gon' do his appearance. That nigga foul!"

"Don't worry 'bout it. We'll find you another hot chick. We in Miami. This the right city to find a last minute bad bitch."

"I hear you but that shit fucked up. We had a usable bad bitch right here and that cocky ass nigga fucked it up. Plus I like the fact that homegirl's face is familiar from being photographed everywhere with Sway but at the same time don't nobody really know who she is. I'm tempted to go to his crib and let him know how foul he is."

"You know where he stays?"

"Of course. He got a condo at the Setai right there on South Beach."

"I tell you what. Since I'm invested in your success, I want you to win. I'll go over there and have a conversation with him myself."

"And say what?"

"You the talent, there's no need for you to worry about things like that. I'll take care of it."

"Cool, make it happen."

When I pulled up to the condo section of the Setai on 101 20 St. I had only one mission and there wasn't a doubt in my mind that I would pull it off. I stood outside the entrance for a long time talking on my cell phone, strictly observing the incoming and outgoing traffic. I figured at some point Sway and Dior would make an appearance. After thirty minutes of bullshit talking on the phone I finagled my way into the lobby which wasn't too difficult given my clean cut appearance and the Lambo I pulled up in. Around the ten minute mark, I saw Dior, Sway, some other female and his bodyguards walking towards The Grill restaurant. I played it cool as I gained headway. When I got somewhat close, I coughed loudly hoping to get Dior's attention. But the only one that turned in my direction to see where the noise was coming from was the unrecognizable female. Everybody else kept all attention in the forward direction.

It wasn't until we all got into the restaurant and the hostess was about to seat them did Dior so happen to turn around and meet my gaze. I felt the reason she turned in my direction was because she could feel my eyes burning a hole through her back. She glanced at me, then turned back around and suddenly glanced back as if trying to peg my familiar face. When she did it a second time, I smiled then discreetly gestured my finger for her to come here. Her demeanor didn't change in one way or another so when she walked off following behind Sway and the rest of his people to the table I didn't know if she was coming back to hear what I had to say or not.

About five minutes later when I saw her go in the direction of the bathroom, I knew she was interested in what I had to say.

"Are you stalking me?" were the first words out of her mouth when I walked up on her.

"No, but by your actions you're letting me know that you don't have a problem with it if I am."

"Don't flatter yourself. I was just curious to know why the man I gave the brush off at the club last night was now in the same spot I'm staying at."

"It's simple. I have something I want to give you."

"Damn, we on that dumb shit again. Didn't I tell you I ain't interested in whatever little money you throwing around?"

"It ain't about money."

"Then what? And please hurry up before Sway sends one of his workers over here to see what is taking me so long."

"I want you to come tomorrow so you can be the lead in Phenomenon's new video."

"Phenomenon...how you know him?" I knew she couldn't have been paying attention last night when I came over to sit at Phenomenon's booth but that was cool.

"Don't worry 'bout all that. I know with a swiftness you was raising your hand to take over the open role so now I'm here to let you know it's available if you want it."

"Damn right I want it but since you know so much about what went down, then you're well aware Sway made it clear that shit wasn't happening."

"I thought you were a girl that made your own rules. You did turn me down because you felt Sway was the one that would bring you fame. Well the way that shit went down earlier today, it ain't gon' never happen up under his thumb."

"So you want me to believe that you have enough clout to get me the lead on the video although Sway made it clear to the director he wasn't going for it."

"Now you're following me."

"I don't know, Sway is totally against that shit. Then I would have to figure out how to be away from him all day tomorrow."

"Either you want fame or you don't. You and I both know that if you're cast as the leading lady in this video the doors will open up for that to happen."

"Still, we both know videos don't pay shit and it's hardly going to be a vehicle to make me financially independent. I'll be taking the chance of Sway cutting me off permanently."

"It's up to you. Last night you were hoopin' and hollerin' that money wasn't what you were after but instead you wanted fame. I'm giving you a chance to make that a reality."

"I understand all that but this shit is much more complicated than that."

"Well you figure it out but here take this," I said handing her one of my business cards. "There are very few liable prospects in life. When one comes banging at your front door you best take it because it may never come again."

The expression on Dior's face said everything—she desperately wanted the fame but she didn't want to lose her mill ticket Sway to get there.

"I'll think about it but what are you getting out of this?"

"I do some business with Phenomenon and he wants you in the video so I'm trying to make it happen."

"I find it hard to believe that is the sole reason you're doing this."

"Maybe I'm also out to prove that if you fuck wit' me I can truly give you what you want. Unlike some people I have no desire to block your dreams if anything I want to make them a reality. So like I said, think about it. But remember you would need to be on set tomorrow morning. The choice is yours. Now go enjoy your meal because we don't want you to keep Sway waiting."

I wasn't sure if I got through to Dior or not. But whatever her decision was I got into her head and made her think about some shit. So whether she showed up tomorrow or not I knew we would eventually meet again.

Dior

It Was Worth It

Flashing Lights by Kanye West was blasting through the speakers in Sway's NYC penthouse and I found myself mouthing every word as if he wrote the song personally for me. It didn't help that I was on my fourth glass of champagne and had done a few lines and it was only the middle of the afternoon. I needed something to get me through the freaking day and night though. Two cunts that I absolutely detested were in my presence and they weren't leaving anytime soon. It was bad enough that happy ho Lori was here but so was this chick Tracy. Tracy rubbed me the wrong way but for a different reason than Lori.

See Tracy started fucking around with Sway a few months before me. He never made her his main girl but clearly he liked the pussy enough that he kept her on a bi-monthly rotation. Most of the females he dealt with were lucky to get a follow-up after the first night but Tracy managed to put herself in the jump-off category, which made her irritating ass think she was somewhat special. No she wasn't getting the red carpet treatment, endless access to designer clothes or jet setting around the world but she was getting some semi consistent dick from Sway which in her mind put her in an elite club. But for me she was just another ho working my nerves.

"Sway said get dressed because you all have someplace to be in an hour," I heard a female voice scream out. Clearly she was trying to be heard over the loud ass music but she kept on repeating herself. I guess because I kept my eyes closed the entire time and she was waiting for me to acknowledge her ass. Finally I complied because as high as I was, I couldn't take her screeching voice any longer.

"I heard you," I said, slightly opening my eyes. But the female kept standing right in front of me practically begging for my undivided attention. "I said I heard you, now move!"

"Don't yell at me. I'm only doing what Sway told me to do." I had to completely open my eyes to see which dumbass female was fucking up my high. Of course it had to be Tracy. She was feeling all sorts of bold leaning forward topless with nothing but some leopard print boy shorts on. She had both hands on her hips as if advertising to say, I have a body shaped like a coke bottle.

"I see you and I hear you, Tracy. Now run off like a good ho and tell Sway you've fulfilled his request."

"You think you such hot shit. I can't wait for Sway to kick yo' uppity ass to the curb."

"Well until he does get the hell out of my face before you completely destroy what's left of my high," I said, swatting my hand, letting Tracy know I needed her gone like ten minutes ago.

As I was about to finish drinking the rest of my champagne I noticed I had ten missed calls and seven text messages on my iPhone. The music had been so loud I figured I didn't hear it ringing.

I didn't even bother to check the voice messages. I just checked out the text and one really caught my interest.

Bitch u rock! U said u'd be a star...u on the way. U on all the blogs!

At first I didn't know what this text was all about. I put my champagne down, realizing if I wanted to get my thoughts together I didn't need to add anymore liquor to my system. Then it all started coming to me quickly. *Oh shit, the video must've dropped! Nobody even gave me a heads up. But the director did say they were keeping it under-wraps until it officially dropped. But that dude Lorenzo promised he would call and let me know. It has been almost a month since I did it so yeah, I should've known it was coming out soon. Fuck! I never got around to telling Sway. That nigga gon' spazz out. I'll work it out.* As all these thoughts started swarming my head, they completely came to a halt when I heard this thunderous crash. It was so fucking loud that it made the music playing sound low.

"Turn that music the fuck off!" I saw Sway standing pointing his finger with big chunks of broken glass surrounding him.

Oh shit, he knows!

"You disobedient hard-headed bitch!"

"Sway, I can explain."

"When the fuck did you do it?" I debated for a quick sec did I tell him the truth or lie.

"When we were in Miami but baby you need to calm down. You don't need to get upset."

"That baby shit ain't gon' work this time, Dior. We were together every fuckin' minute of every fuckin' day, so you couldn't have done it while we were there, yo' lying ass. Unless..." I could tell his mind was backtracking. "Unless, when early that next morning you said you had to catch the first flight out to Philly because you had just got word your mother was mad sick was some bullshit? Did yo' scheming ass make that shit up?"

It had been so long that I had forgotten that was the story I used to get the fuck away from Sway and get my ass on the video set. At the time it was the best excuse I could come up with, now it had me looking all sorts of trifling. I swallowed hard before answering. "Baby, calm down." I stood up and walked over to Sway and stroked the side of his face like I had done on so many other instances but my luck had ran out because I didn't get the usual response.

"Bitch, don't touch me," Sway barked, knocking me down on the cold marble floor. "I told you I didn't want you doing that fuckin' video. Not only did you disobey me but you got me lookin' like a punk 'cause you went behind my back after I told everybody on set you belonged to me and you wasn't doin' that shit."

"Sway, you blowing this outta proportion. Ain't nobody thinking that shit! It's a fuckin' music video."

"Yeah, that yo' thirsty ass had to be in. I hope it was worth it 'cause I'm done wit' yo' no good ass. Get yo' shit and get the fuck out my crib."

"Baby, you don't mean that. You can't be done wit' me over a video!"

"Do you know who the fuck I am! Don't nobody disrespect me especially not some ho that I put on the map! Now get yo' shit and get the fuck outta here. Fuck that! You ain't walking outta here wit' none of that shit I bought you. If you not on my arm you ain't even worthy. Tracy, give Dior the clothes you came in."

I watched as Tracy hurried off to retrieve her clothes. She quickly returned and tossed them at me, thrilled to give me her hand me downs. She and Lori both stared at me with glowing smirks on their faces. They had been waiting for me to fall and felt no need to hide their enthusiasm of witnessing it firsthand. The same bodyguards that use to sniff after me like I was Queen of the world were now standing over me waiting for me to put on the clothes Tracy threw in my direction so they could escort me out.

With the glare of disdain coming from Sway I didn't bother to further try and plea my case. He had a point to make and unfortunately it was at my expense. So instead of fighting against it I took what little I had and left.

When I got to my apartment, I flopped down on the couch and ripped off the clothes I had no choice but to put on unless I wanted to walk down the street naked. Knowing I had been force to wear Tracy's clothes made me feel disgusting and cheap. I tossed them in the trashcan feeling slightly vindicated. As I walked back over to the couch it felt somewhat good to be back home in my own crib. It definitely wasn't close to being in Sway's penthouse or his condo or his mansion but at least it was my shit that nobody could throw me out of and truth be told it was actually cute.

It was a one bedroom on the upper west side and when I first got it you couldn't tell me shit. But when you start getting accustomed to living Sway's lifestyle a place like this makes you feel like you're two steps away from being in the poorhouse. Not wanting to focus on my misery I picked up the remote control and there was Phenomenon on 106 and Park about to debut his new video. I sat up and for the first time within the last couple of hours I was excited.

"Wow, I look fuckin' amazing!" I said out loud as the video played. They had my makeup, hair and clothes all on point. The quality of the video was top notch too, no low budget shit going on. Then the scene came where I was wearing the gray lace bra and panty set. They had a shot of me standing, capturing a side angle but my face was looking directly into the camera. It was right before I walked over to the bed Phenomenon was waiting for me in. The way I straddled the nigga you would've thought we really fucked and I was sure Sway was thinking the exact thing. The very idea of that made me smile. He tossed me out in the street like I was yesterday's trash. He needed to think that maybe

I was somebody else's treasure. Seeing myself up there on the television screen killing it made me decide that I had made the right decision doing the video. Yeah I had lost Sway but if I worked my shit right it would gain me so much more.

Lorenzo

Whatever You Want

★⋆★⋆★⋆★⋆

"Yo, the streets is going wild over your new video."

"I know it's crazy. I had no idea that niggas and bitches love to see you get lovey dovey wit' a fly ass chick. If I knew I would get this kinda love, I woulda came wit' this from the jump!"

"Nah, you did the right thing going hard on your first joint. You need to always get them with that grimy shit off the cuff, that's the only way you'll get that respect from the hood. Then when you come back with that mellow shit everybody else gon' jump on board."

"Yo, Lorenzo, I think you right. If I had done

this joint first they would see me strictly as a soft nigga, now I got them across the board."

"Now you get my point," I said, nodding my head as I sat in my car talking to Phenomenon on the phone.

"No doubt. And that was a damn good look you getting me that chick Dior. I don't know how you pulled that shit off. You know Sway dumped her behind that shit," Phenomenon chuckled.

"Get the fuck outta here!"

"I'm serious!"

"How you know?"

"The nigga called me the same day the video dropped. First he was like, how you gon' disrespect me like that using my girl in the video when you knew I wasn't down for the shit. I explained it was a business move and that was all. We was pressed for time and thought she was a fit for the job."

"What did he say when you told him that?"

"That nigga wasn't tryna here that shit. He was acting like what he say go and that I fucked up our relationship by disrespecting him the way I did. But our so called relationship was already dead when his punk ass bolted from my video set without even doing his guest spot."

"But you still didn't tell me how you know he not wit' Dior no more."

"Oh, 'cause before he hung up the phone, he said some slick shit like, I know you fucked her and you can have her cause I don't want her tainted pussy no more."

"Word, that nigga said that."

"Sure did...that nigga crazy! Of course I didn't let his stupid ass know otherwise but I was thinking if you let that bad bitch go 'cause you thought I got the pussy then you a fool." I listened as Phenomenon laughed, getting a kick at Sway's reaction to the situation. My thoughts instantly went to how Dior was coping with it. On one hand she was on the tip of everybody's tongue 'cause there was no denying homegirl was looking like the only thing smoking right now but on the flipside she lost what she considered her biggest asset—Sway. I figured it was the perfect time to make another move. I knew she was probably feeling anxious to make sure she stayed in the spotlight. If she hadn't already, soon she would be scheming to find her next victim to stay relevant.

"That Sway cat is a piece of work. I guess everything they say about that nigga is true."

"Yeah, and then some. I hope I don't ever start feeling myself to that point. He probably got a kiss my ass at all time contract you must sign before being a part of his inner circle." We were both laughing after Phenomenon said that shit because it was highly likely there was some truth to it.

"You ain't got to worry, I won't let you."

"I know that's right!"

"So where you at now?"

"In Atl. I'm performing at some club tonight. You know they got me doing mad club dates and shit before my album drop."

"Yeah, I know. That road shit is draining but it's gon' pay off, watch when them first week numbers come in."

"True, but yo, whatever I gotta do. I've been wantin' this shit for so long that if I have to live on the road for the next two years to blow up and get this fame shit then that's what I'll do. Ain't no turning back now."

When Phenomenon said that, my mind again went back to Dior because she too craved that exact same fame. I wanted to call her as soon as I got off the phone with Phenomenon but I had been parked outside Lala's crib for awhile and I saw her peeping out her window a few times. It would be rude to keep having long ass conversations when she knew I was basically right at her front door.

"I know you gon' handle yo' shit tonight so I'll hit you up tomorrow."

"That works, man." When I hung up with Phenomenon I went straight to Lala's door. She had it open before I even made it to the top stair.

"I was starting to wonder if you were ever coming in," Lala smiled.

"Sorry 'bout that. I was handling some business."

"Aren't you always? With all the work you do I hope you make some time for fun. That was something Darnell rarely did. You seem to be just like him in that way and now he's gone. You can't make up for lost time Lorenzo."

"Don't compare me to Darnell."

"I wasn't doing that." I could see the startled reaction on Lala's face because of what I said. "But would it be so bad if I was? Darnell was your friend."

"I just don't like to be compared to other people, friend or no friend. So where is Tania?" I asked trying to skip over this topic. Hearing that nigga's name still put me in a bad mood and that was no fault of Lala.

"My mom took her to a birthday party."

"The last few times I've been here she's always gone, Tania's schedule busier than mine." I was able to put a smile on Lala's face with my comment which I was happy about. I tried to avoid any sort of conversation about Darnell because I loathed him but that was something Lala could never know. No matter what she always managed to make him a part of our discussion. It concerned me that soon there would come a point that I wouldn't be able to conceal my contempt for him.

"Maybe you should consider calling ahead of time so we can plan for your arrival instead of just popping up," Lala suggested.

"I never thought about it but you might be

right."

"I am. I'm sure Tania would love if you came over and had dinner with us and so would I. You've done so much for us I want to do something for you."

"I told you, Lala, you don't owe me nothing."

"I know that but I like when you come by. I enjoy your company. I guess what I'm trying to say is that you don't have to just stop by when you're dropping off money. You're welcome anytime."

For the first time I paid close attention at the way Lala looked at me. I couldn't lie and say that the last few times I came by I got some sort of vibe from her but the thought went as fast as it came. But there was no denying now that the vibe was real.

Lala had her hair pulled back off her face with nothing to hide what was going on behind her eyes. Her face was almost angelic like Tania's except she wasn't a child she was a grown woman with sexual appeal. As fine as Lala was, I didn't want to go there. I could see the shit getting messy for a few reasons and I didn't need any of them in my life.

"I have to be going but let Tania know I stopped by and I'll be back to see her soon," I said, putting my usual envelope full of money on the table.

"I will and I hope you'll consider my offer for dinner," Lala responded by putting her hand on top of mine as I sat the envelope down.

"I'll consider it."

"That's all I'm asking, Lorenzo." I knew

Lala was asking for a lot more but since I had no intentions in complying with any of it I left it alone.

"I'll see you later, Lala." I could hear her saying something but I blocked it out as I made my exit. It was easy for me to erase what had just happened from my mind because I immediately dialed Dior's number as I was headed to my car.

"Hello," she answered in a curious voice. I knew she didn't recognize the number so I was glad she picked up.

"What's up, Dior."

"Who is this?"

"Lorenzo."

"Lorenzo! I been waiting for you to call me. What happened to you giving me a heads up before the video dropped...huh?"

"I apologize. I got caught up in some shit and honestly it slipped my mind. But you came out looking like a star so it's all good."

"That ain't the point. You was supposed to give me time to get shit straight with Sway."

"You right. Again, I apologize but as savvy as you are I'm sure you smoothed things over with him," I said pretending not to know that Sway had dismissed her.

"So what do you want, Lorenzo?"

"Checking up on you, seeing how shit was poppin' now that you were a star."

"Star, hum if you say so," she answered sarcastically.

"I know yo' phone been ringing off the hook since the video came out."

"Nope, just the opposite. I believe Sway's petty ass shut all that shit down."

"You might be right 'cause everybody buzzin' 'bout that video and especially you. But don't sweat that. What I'm about to tell you will no doubt put a smile on your face."

"It will?" she asked as if in complete shock.

"Yep. This should make up for me forgetting to call you about the video in advance."

"What is it...tell me!" her voice had now gone from having a pissed off attitude to hopeful excitement.

"They're going to shoot you to be on the next cover of King Magazine."

"Stop lyin'!"

"I ain't lyin'."

"The cover, not some inside one page booty shot?"

"Nope, that would be takin' a step back. How you gon' go from lead of Phenomenon's new video to that. It's the cover, baby."

"Don't play, Lorenzo! How the fuck did you manage that?"

"Money can do wonders, everybody gotta price."

"I can't believe you did that for me."

"Dior, I told you whatever you want. You think you need Sway to get to the top but money can get you there just as fast if not faster."

"Sway ain't even a factor anymore."

"Why is that?"

"After the video dropped he dumped me."

"Wow, just like that. That nigga cold blooded."

"Are you serious about that cover?"

"Yeah, why you ask?"

"'Cause that will show Sway's ass. I'ma personally make sure he gets a copy of that shit so he can choke on it."

"Yo you crazy!" I laughed.

"Maybe, but I'm serious. You have no idea all the bullshit I put up with dealing with him and then you should've seen how he dumped me. After shit wasn't jumping off for me, I started to regret doing the fuckin' video. But after the news you just gave me, I'm back in business."

"Yes, you are. I'll be in touch with all the details so keep yo' head up."

"Will do!"

Before Dior hung up the phone I could hear the fight back in her voice. I could tell she didn't want to admit it but getting dumped by Sway had left her shook. She had grown dependent on that jet set life with him and it all slipped away in a matter of seconds. But I was going to enjoy playing a major part in helping her dreams come true. It was actually turning out to be a lot more amusing than I thought it would be. Initially I didn't even think of it as being fun. Part of me wanted to prove to Dior that my money could be as powerful as Sway's fame in getting her what she wanted and the other part of me wanted to get her in bed since she said that wasn't a possibility. But what was viewed to me as a game in the beginning was now turning into a challenge of how far I could take this fame thing and would I win at it.

Dior

So Amazing

✦★✦🟊✦★✦

When the cab dropped me off in front of the Gramercy Park Hotel, I knew Brittani would be pissed that I was almost thirty minutes late. Luckily we were meeting at the Maialino for lunch, so it wasn't a doubt in my mind that there had to be a wait. If she was seated it only could've happened within the last five to ten minutes.

"I'm meeting someone," I said, bypassing the long line and the hostess as I noticed Brittani sitting in a corner table. "Sorry I'm late, sweetie," I smiled before sitting down.

"Dior, I've known you long enough to know that this is on time for you, plus we only got a table a few minutes ago."

"Yeah, I figured that. Everybody is always raving about how great the food is here."

"It really is. It's my new favorite spot. I hope you don't mind but I already ordered. I know what's best on the menu. But enough about the food, how are you holding up?"

"How do you think?" I asked in my most cynical voice. "A couple weeks ago I was in Paris now I can barely afford French fries."

"It's that bad?" Brittani's mouth was wide open waiting for my reply.

"Pretty much, so I hope this meal is on you."

"You don't have money for food, Dior? You didn't save any money while you were with Sway?"

"Please, the most cash Sway ever put in my hand was to tip people. He covered all my expenses and gave me access to his credit cards. I figured by the time our relationship was over I would be so hot people would pay me to show up to places and do things. But it hasn't worked out that way."

"Even after that video you did with Phenomenon? That's the number one song and video out right now. I'd think your phone would be blowing up!"

"Me too! I swear I believe Sway called everybody and their mother after he dumped me letting them know not to fuck with me at all."

"Seriously, is dude that petty...wait, I forgot

we are talking about Sway."

"He's so foul," I said, shaking my head.

"So what are you gonna to do? I mean you don't have anybody that can help you out until you get back on your feet?"

"No, Sway made sure I cut everybody off when I started dealing with him. I do have something brewing that would put me in the center of shit if it happens. But I'm not sure if it's legit or not."

"What is it?"

"I don't want to talk about it because if it don't happen I'll be beyond fuckin' pissed and if it does happen then you'll know about it like everybody else."

"Cool, but again, what are you going to do for money, some more videos?"

"Hell no! You know that shit don't pay no damn money. I did the one with Phenomenon because I thought the exposure would open so many doors for me, which would mean making some money!"

"I can always hook you up with an athlete. You know they love video girls."

"Unless it was Kobe Bryant, who is married, so that's not gonna happen, why would I date some random athlete. Seriously, how do you go from like one of the biggest hip hop artist to some regular NBA player? That's not gonna garner me consistent media attention. If anything people will say I'm desperate and a has been. I refuse to be the next

Amber Rose."

"Since I know you're not gonna go out and get a real job, you have to date somebody to get your bills paid."

"True, but it has to be the right man. They say the next person you date has to be equal or better than the last one."

"Unless I missed the announcement, Jay Z is still married so your options are limited."

"No shit Sherlock."

"Don't get upset with me because you're in this predicament. When we first left Philly and we moved here in search of fame and fortune, well you fame me fortune I told you to find a rich man and get pregnant. That way you would always know you had a steady check coming in."

"Brittani, that is so 2000. You and I both know that just like an NFL contract that money ain't guaranteed."

"I'm a NBA baby mama and I ain't had a problem paying a bill yet. So it's worked for me."

"So far, let's reconvene this conversation in a few years and see if you're talking the same shit."

"I bet you I will!"

"Look at Nas and Kelis. I know she wasn't counting on getting her payments sliced in half. And I guarantee you in six months to a year, Nas will be right back in front of a judge, screaming we still in a recession, getting it reduced some more.

But honestly Brittani, I'm not trying to rain on your parade. Real talk, I hope your shit continues to work out for you but you know I never wanted to do the baby mama thing. I don't want to be known for poppin' out some kid for a famous person. I want my own fame."

"I hear you but fame don't pay the bills—money does, something you don't seem to have. You need to figure out something, Dior, and quick."

"You think I don't know that. I don't even have money to pay for my meal. So again, I hope those child support checks keep coming in on time because I might need a small loan to hold me over."

"You know I'll do whatever I can for you but I really think you need to let me set you up, even if it's just a short fling."

"I don't know, Brittani. Athletes aren't big on trickin' money unless you're a stripper. And that's only because they like to show off by throwing money around in front of other men in the club to boost their ego."

"Maybe you won't get any cash out the deal but you will get some bills paid and definitely a few meals."

"I came so far from when we first got here and we were sharing that studio in Harlem. Now I'm back at square one. Do you know, Sway didn't even let me keep any of the clothes, shoes, bags or jewelry he got me. When I was getting dressed today and I looked in my closet, everything is last season. Maybe I should've taken my mother's advice and stayed in school after all." I looked down and began shaking my head thinking about how much my life had changed in such a short period of time."

"Dior, you have to stop feeling sorry for yourself. Growing up we were so poor we didn't even know what designer shit was. And chillin' on a yacht or flying in a jet, hell we had never even been on a plane. So yeah, you have come a long way. Right now shit is bad for you, but you've seen worse. If you let Sway kill all your dreams then he wins. You'll get through this. Now no more misery talk. Here comes our food, so enjoy because honestly we don't know when you'll get another meal." We both fell out laughing before devouring our food.

Later on that evening as I sat at home warming up leftovers from the meal I had earlier in the day, I replayed the conversation I had with Brittani in my mind. I had to stop feeling sorry for myself and move forward. So what if Sway dumped me. That was a risk I had already come to terms with when Lorenzo brought the opportunity back to me. Regretting my decision and thinking of what might have been was serving me no purpose. The only thing I needed to do was figure out a master plan. If Lorenzo really delivered on what he said he could then I knew things would without a doubt shift in my favor. But there was a small fraction of me that felt he was full of shit. I mean I had flat out turned him down all in the name of Sway so why would he want to help me. I had played the game long enough to realize that all men loved a challenge and being told 'no' fit in that category, especially for a man like Lorenzo. I didn't know much about him but judging from his good looks alone he didn't hear that word often from a woman. So that could well be the reason, he was trying to buy the pussy without actually handing over the cash and paying for it. Whatever the reason I didn't fucking care as long as it worked out in my favor. As I continued trying to figure shit out in my head I heard my cell ringing. I saw Brittani's name on the screen.

"What's up?"

"Get dressed. I have a party for us to go to."

"Girl, I don't feel like going to no damn party. I ain't got nothing to celebrate."

"Well you ain't gon' never have nothing to celebrate if you keep yo' ass in that damn apartment. Can't nobody find you in there."

"Whose party is it?"

"The Knicks and Miami are playing tomorrow night so Lebron James is having a party."

"I can't stand that egotistical mutherfucka. I

don't wanna go to his party."

"Lebron is cool people, but you ain't got to like him to go to the party. Everybody will be there so it'll be a good look. Plus, you need to be seen. You don't want people to think you went into hiding because you ain't with Sway no more."

"True, but I don't even think I got any hot shit to wear. Wait, I did have this dress that Sway got me that I left over here and never got a chance to wear. Bingo!"

"Cool, I'll pick you up in about an hour so hurry up. Bye!"

"Damn, when you said an hour, you really meant an hour," I said shutting the passenger door.

"You know it's gone be ridiculous in there and I want to make sure we posted up in our spot, especially with that bad ass dress you got on. Is that leather on the sleeve cuffs?"

"Yep, it has leather going down the v-neck collar and the belt too."

"I ain't never seen that dress, who make that?"

"Gucci. I can't believe I almost forgot about it. But what happened was that Sway's stylist had dropped it off because I was supposed to wear it to some party with Sway but I didn't make it back home so I ended up wearing something else and it's been sitting in my closet. But I remembered at the perfect time."

"Yo Sway's stylist got some good fuckin' taste 'cause that shit is sick."

"Yeah he does. And I ain't got none of it."

"How you lose all your clothes?"

"I was basically living with Sway so all my clothes were at his different cribs. So when he gave me my walking papers, it ain't like he had the shit shipped to me."

"Wow, that's got to be devastating," Brittani said, shaking her head.

"Pretty much but ain't shit I can do about it so fuck it!"

"Don't worry, tonight all that is gonna change. We gon' find you a new cat."

"You keep talking 'bout hooking me up and not both of us finding a new man, so shit must be real good with you and Kevin."

"He been acting right lately. I ain't caught him in no bullshit so he must be keeping the groupies in check."

"Do you see yourself going from baby mama to wife in the near future?"

"I ain't say all that," Brittani smiled, turning on West 23rd Street. "If we do get married I know it ain't gon' be no time soon which is cool with me as long as the checks keep clearing and the bitches stay out my way."

"I don't know how you baby mamas do it.

Always jumping through hoops trying to make sure you keep the other hoes away."

"That shit is a full time job but at least I'm not like that dumbass Priscilla."

"What the hell she do now?"

"You didn't see how she released all those bootleg pictures to the blogs?"

"Since I know I ain't been featured on them lately, I haven't been checking the blogs."

"Well her and Ross and all their kids had been on a yacht for they family vacation. Well on a daily basis from the beginning to the end of their trip this heffa was giving us a play by play photo update of them out. And Ross didn't even look like he wanted to touch her ass. She tried to make it look like it was paparazzi candid shots but everybody know that silly ho takes one of her best friends who is a photographer on all her trips with Ross to take pics and send them to the blogs."

"Stop playing!"

"I wish I was but it's that serious for her."

"But he ain't even with Priscilla no more, he go with that young girl Jessica. When I would be at the parties with Sway, I would always see them together."

"That's my point. We know he is with Jessica and so does Priscilla but she tries to use Ross spending time with his kids as a pathetic opportunity to make it seem like he still her man."

"Oh I get it. That's her way of trying to keep the groupies away."

"Exactly, but Priscilla need to give it up because unfortunately for her Jessica is no groupie. Ross live with that girl. But Priscilla stay trying to use them kids and Ross being her baby daddy as a way to stay relevant and gain some attention."

"That's what I was telling you earlier, I don't want to be one of those having a baby for a famous dude so I can be somebody types."

"I don't want to be one of those either. I don't have to nor want to be in the spotlight. I just want me and my child to be very well taken care of. But when you're like Priscilla, desperate for some fame, dropping a bunch of babies and still not making it to wife status you start making us all look stupid. I wish she would go sit her tired ass down somewhere and concentrate on raising her kids. She is too old for that bullshit. If she ain't got the ring and walked down the aisle by now it's time to give it up."

"Girl, that's why I got to hurry and get my shit together before my time be up! I'm sure Priscilla never thought she'd be forty with four kids and still a baby mama."

"Dior, you're only twenty-four, you've got plenty of time."

"They were all twenty-four at one time too. It seems like yesterday we were eighteen coming to New York. Time don't stop."

"I never thought about it that way. But you're right. It seems like yesterday Destiny was born and now she's about to be three."

"I know shit is sweet with Kevin right now but I hope you're working on a contingency plan. It's one thing to be like me, broke and single. It's another being broke with a child."

"Girl, we about to go into this party, I don't need the headache right now. We can discuss this on another day, preferably over a bottle of wine."

"I feel you. Let's go, the party awaits us!"

"Thank goodness you know that dude at the door," I sighed, as we pushed our way through the crowd of people trying to get in the club.

"I wouldn't have come if I didn't. You know these types of shindigs be mad tight. Here, put on this vip wristband or we'll be stuck with the regular people out here," Brittani said, handing it to me. We maneuvered our way straight to the back where there was nothing but beefed up bodyguards and rope. There was a row of booths that were predominantly filled with NBA players. In front of each booth there was your obvious treasure hunters all dolled up in their best attire hoping they would catch a baller's attention.

"Where are we going?" I finally asked not wanting to be standing amongst the other thirsty looking women.

"Right here," Brittani stated before sitting down.

"You have a booth?"

"Why you look so surprised?"

"Because I am! How did you manage to get a booth?"

"Bitch, don't play. It's first class all the way. We can't be up in a Lebron James party like we some low budget groupies. How am I gon' score you a baller if we don't look like we ballin' ourselves!"

"Brittani, you are truly my girl! I'm so glad I came out tonight...I needed this!"

"Yes you do. Now sit back, we 'bout to pop some bottles." And that's exactly what we did for the first hour of the party. We arrived at the perfect time where it wasn't too crowded but it damn sure wasn't empty. We were positioned in the ideal spot to watch as more and more people came through. Of course everybody was trying to get in the vip area especially the women. That was to be expected since that was where all the money was at. What made where we were sitting so great was that as packed as the rest of the club got the vip section remained uncongested.

"Hey, aren't you that girl from the Phenomenon video?"

"Yes," I smiled politely.

"If one more nigga ask you that question, I'ma put a sign on our table stating, 'Yes this is the hot girl from the video.'"

"You so silly!"

"I ain't silly, they silly. This section ain't but so big so I know they've seen the guy before them and the other guy before and so on coming up to you. But they keep asking the same dumb question." We both were laughing because the shit was true. "Oh, and look who just showed up, your leading man."

I turned in the direction Brittani was looking at and I saw Phenomenon and a couple of his friends sit down at the booth across from us. When he caught a glimpse of my face he put his hand up motioning for me to come over to his table.

"I do not feel like going over to his table."

"Girl, go over there and speak to him. It's a good look for you. All the guys will be able to get a clear view of you in that bad ass dress and you'll start a bidding war up in this mutherfucka."

"Brittani, you ain't got no sense. I'll be right back."

"Take your time. 'Cause all these dudes 'bout to start coming over to our table wanting to know how to get at you. While you're gone I'll be putting them in the potential pile or garbage pile."

I shook my head and made my way towards Phenomenon. When I got a few feet away I felt somebody reach for my arm. I was about to snap thinking it was some thirsty dude but when I turned I laid eyes on a familiar looking female's face.

"Aren't you the girl from Phenomenon's new video?"

"Yes." I was eyeing her crazy because I was thinking to myself this chick can't be a fan. It's a music video for goodness sakes.

"I thought that was you. Hi, I'm Courtney. I was supposed to do the video." She gave me this cute smile and instantly I remembered her and that's why she looked familiar. "You looked so pretty in the video. When I saw you I regretted not wanting to wear the lingerie. I thought it would come across as distasteful but seeing you in it made me realize that it didn't."

"I'm Dior and thank you." Her genuine sweetness totally threw me the fuck off, the same way it did that day I saw her at the video shoot.

"You welcome. I know everybody probably wants to talk to you so I won't keep you. I just wanted you to know that you were awesome in the video and since somebody had to replace me I'm glad it was you."

"Thanks again...but listen, don't regret not doing the video. You should never do something you're not comfortable with. The right project will come along and it'll be perfect for you."

"You think so?"

"I know so."

"Dior, you saying that means so much to me. I thought I had ruined my chances of breaking in this industry but now you've given me hope."

"If you don't mind me asking, how old are you,

Courtney?"

"Eighteen."

"Wow, that's how old I was when I came to New York. You'll be fine just stay focused."

"I will. I thought you would be so stuck up but you're a sweetheart," she gushed.

"Now that's a word I've never heard anybody use to describe me," I giggled. "You're the first and I'm sure you'll be the last. I gotta go but have fun tonight."

"You too and thanks. Hopefully we'll run into each other again," I heard Courtney say as I made my way to Phenomenon. I was ready to get away from Courtney because I couldn't comprehend it but I had some sort of soft spot for her that made me uncomfortable.

"Damn, Ma, I know you a celebrity now but why you gotta keep a dude waiting so long," Phenomenon said when I got to his table.

"You got jokes, we know you the only real celebrity up in here."

"Not no more," he shot back, using his chin to point over my shoulder. I turned around and saw Sway headed in our direction. To my disgust he had four chicks with him and one of them was Tracy.

"I see you took me up on my suggestion and started fuckin' my leftovers," Sway snarled.

"Sway man, I told you it wasn't like that," Phenomenon shot back.

"You ain't gotta lie to me."

"Exactly. So if I said it ain't happenin' then it must be true. 'Cause like you said, I ain't got to lie to you," Phenomenon popped, letting Sway know he had no fear of him.

"Is that the dress I bought?" I guess since Sway couldn't get a rise from Phenomenon he opted to start fucking with me.

"I don't know what you're talkin' 'bout."

"You can't afford no Gucci dress so don't act like you don't know where it came from and who bought it."

"Sway, what is your point?"

"Take that shit off now! I paid for it, I want it back."

"You're a lunatic, Sway. Phenomenon, I'm going back to my table. We'll talk later."

"No doubt, I'll be over there to you as soon as some people move out the way," he said mean mugging Sway.

"Excuse me," I said trying to walk past Sway.

"You heard what I said, take off my dress."

"I ain't takin' off nothing. I don't fuck wit' you no more so talk that shit to one of these silly hoes," I barked, pointing my finger in his female companion's direction.

"Bitch, don't call me no ho," Tracy barked back.

"Trick, shut the fuck up talkin' to me. This nigga ain't even got you in no new shit. You wearing an outfit my pussy done sweated up in. Now all of you move out my fuckin' way." I brushed past them, daring one of those heffas to breathe on me. I was ready to step out my five inch heels and put an old school beat down on one of them bitches.

"Dior, what the hell happened? I was over here taking down names and numbers for you. Next thing I know, I look up and see Sway and his gang of bitches looking like they 'bout to tar and feather you."

"Girl please, Sway is such a diva," I said rolling my eyes.

"Well get ready for round two because here he comes again."

"Damn, this nigga ain't even giving me a chance to sit down and take a break! Sway, what do you want?" I huffed as soon as he walked up on me.

"Since you don't want to give back what belongs to me then I'll ruin it for you."

"Excuse me, what the hell..." Before I could complete my sentence my face and entire body was being drenched in champagne. Everybody in the vip section stood frozen in astonishment. The only voices I heard was Sway's gaggle of bitches laughing at what he had just done to me.

"Now I bet you wish you would've taken that dress off when I told you to," were Sway's departing words before emptying the rest of the champagne on me and walking off.

"Dior, I can't believe Sway did that. Come sit down," Brittani suggested but I couldn't move. I was cold, wet and fucking embarrassed.

"Dior, are you ok? Put this on." Phenomenon wrapped his coat around me but I still felt like shit. "That's a foul nigga right there. He got issues fo' real yo."

"Come on, Dior, we're leaving," Brittani said grabbing my hand.

"You good, keep my coat. I know I'll see you again."

"Thanks, Phenomenon."

I kept my head down the entire time until we got out the club and reached Brittani's car. I was in complete shock and too many things don't shock me. "I can't believe Sway showed out like that."

"I can. Clearly that nigga still got a hard on for you but instead of admitting he want you back, he want to make you fuckin' miserable. He lowdown fo' real. He's like a spoiled brat. When he doesn't get his way he has all sorts of uncontrollable tantrums. How did you deal wit' that dude for so long? He's worse than a child."

"I know."

"But you still like him don't you?"

"He's like nicotine and you know how hard of a habit that is to break."

"You betta get on the patch or something 'cause that nigga bad news."

Brittani had no idea just how right she was. Sway was so bad for me and being away from him made it more evident. It wasn't only the clothes, jewelry and designer bags I yearned for, it was also the drugs. When I was with him they were always around so I never had to be without it. It didn't feel like a need only a desire. But now that my supply had been cut off I missed it. I had been trying so hard to fight that feeling of weakness from no longer having Sway in my life. But I was beginning to succumb to it and it was scaring the shit out of me.

"Dior, we're here," I heard Brittani yell out. "Are you okay? That was like my third time telling you we're in front of your apartment building."

"Sorry, I have so much on my mind."

"I can only imagine, but try to get some rest. I know I keep telling you this, but it will get better."

"I believe you're right because it can't get any worse. Goodnight, Brittani."

When I woke up the next morning I had a ton of missed calls from Brittani. I figured it was of no importance and she was only calling to check up on me. I was starving but before I could make it to the kitchen my phone began ringing and it was Brittani again.

"I appreciate your concern, Brittani, but I'm okay so you can stop blowing up my phone."

"You must didn't read the paper this morning!"

"Huh?"

"Go to Page Six."

"I don't get the Post."

"Turn on your computer and go online."

"Can't this wait until after I eat? I'm starving!"

"Get on your computer," she demanded. I decided to do what Brittani asked because I figured the sooner I got her off the phone the sooner I could stuff my mouth.

"Oh my fuckin' goodness!" I kept saying over and over again.

"Bitch, you're back on the fuckin' map! You can't pay for that sort of publicity." After I read it to myself like three times I read it out loud.

Maybe Hip Hop Superstar Sway isn't over his former flame Dior after all. Sources say last night at Lebron James's party he worked himself up in a jealous rage when he spotted his ex getting cozy with rising rap star Phenomenon. Sway must have thought that Dior's leading lady role in Phenomenon's new video wasn't just for the cameras. Because he caused the beauty to leave the club after drenching the three thousand dollar dress he bought her in champagne.

"How fuckin' amazing is that? He thought he was ruining your night but all he did was turn it around to work in your favor."

"I can't believe my luck. Maybe something good will finally come out of all this."

"It already has. Everybody in the industry is talking about you right now and what went down at the party. Your stock just skyrocketed."

"I understand all that but I need for this talk to turn into some paying gigs. A bitch is broke!"

"Be a little more patient. The tide is about to turn and soon the money will come."

I so needed that to be true. But Brittani was right. I would be the leading topic for at least the next couple of days. This was the best thing that had happened to me since my breakup with Sway. I needed to keep the momentum going which was difficult especially since I didn't have a publicist to plant bogus stories for me. But shit like that cost money because I didn't know one publicist that worked for free.

When I got off the phone with Brittani I decided to call Lorenzo. Once again his phone rang and then went to voicemail. Unlike the other times I called, this time I decided to leave a voice message. He was making me feel ignored and I hated that. But I wanted to know if this King Magazine cover was legit. It was the only thing brewing for me at the moment. I knew they weren't going to pay me for doing the cover but the exposure would bring in some much needed cash from other sources. I had my fingers crossed so tight that Lorenzo wasn't bullshitting and would get in touch with me soon. I thought I would've heard back from him by now but it was like he just disappeared.

I was pacing back and forth wondering how I could get in touch with him. I meant to ask Phenomenon if he had spoken to Lorenzo but Sway sidetracked me with the show he put on. Oh, how things had changed in less than twenty-four hours. Last night I was embarrassed and pissed but now if I had the money, I would send Sway a bouquet of flowers, thanking him for the unintentional generosity he bestowed upon me.

After printing out the plug in Page Six I taped it on my kitchen wall. I tried calling Lorenzo one last time and since I couldn't get him on the phone, I decided to finally make myself something to eat. Between bites of my veggie omelet and drinking orange juice I continued to read the write up and smile at the same time. For the first time in a while I was feeling good. I turned my music on and brought some much needed life into my apartment.

"Dior, you are on your way," I said out loud as I stood in front of my full length mirror. "No matter how hard he may try, Sway will not be able to stop me. Pretty soon, I'll be back to walking the red carpet in the best designer clothes and it won't be because Sway paid for them. The designers will be giving me clothes for free and will be begging me to wear their shit because I'll give them press. Sway will regret the day he ever dumped me. I'll be on all the blogs, magazines, doing television interviews and it won't be as Sway's girlfriend, it will be because I'm Dior. I'll show Sway and everybody else who thought I wouldn't make it. I will be a star, I will be a star," I repeated over and over again because I felt if I said it enough times, I would convince myself that it would come true.

Lorenzo

Hell Of A Life

★⋆★⋆★⋆

"How is she doing?" I asked the doctor as I watched my mother sitting in her wheelchair staring out the window.

"We feel optimistic that we've found the right combination of medications but of course we won't know for sure until we give it some time."

"Has she started talking at all?"

"No, she's still withdrawn in herself. As I told you before, Mr. Taylor, your mother may never speak again."

I walked in my mother's room and stood next to her but it was as if I wasn't even there. Every time

I would come to visit her the only thing that gave me peace of mind was that the doctor assured me she wasn't in any physical pain but mentally my mother was gone. I didn't know which one felt worse, when she was a drug addict or when she was diagnosed with being schizophrenia.

After her diagnosis I found the best private psychiatric treatment center in the state of New York but in the three years she'd been here instead of getting better she seemed to be fading further away. She went from hallucinations, delusions, disorganized speech to finally not speaking at all. At first I blamed the doctors, nurses anybody but it had nothing to do with them. My mother had been sick for a very long time but nobody noticed because her erratic behavior was blamed on her crack addiction. By the time I found her, my father was dead and I barely recognized her as being the woman that gave birth to me but she was. And even though she had been out of my life since I was a little boy, when I found her again, I still loved her as if she had raised me and never abandoned me.

What I hoped for each time I would visit was that my mother knew I was here and felt my presence. That never seemed to be the case but I think that's what kept me coming back week after week. I was praying one day she would give me a sign that she did. So when she stared out the window I would stare too, wondering in my mind what she was thinking about, if anything at all. Did she notice when it would rain or when the sun would come out; did that make a difference in her mood? Did she appreciate the garden view she had from her room? All these questions I had but I wasn't able to accept I would never know the answers to any of them.

"Yo, what's good?" I answered, as I got in the car leaving my mother's treatment center.

"We have a situation."

"I see. I'm headed back that way, I'll be in touch." I ended the call thinking that I wasn't in the mood for the bullshit today. When I would come see my mother it literally drained all my energy. It would be as if I left it in the room with her. Having to go home and deal with business bullshit wasn't what I needed right now.

"Damn, who the fuck is this?" I moaned feeling the vibration of the phone. I saw Lala's name and remembered I hadn't been by there the last couple of weeks. "What's up, Lala."

"Hey, Lorenzo."

"Is everything ok? You don't sound good."

"Tania's been asking for you. Last time you were here you told me to tell her you would be back soon to visit but you've been a no show."

"I apologize. I've had a lot going on these last couple weeks. I have some business I have to handle tonight but I'll be over there tomorrow afternoon."

"Are you sure? I don't want to tell Tania and then you not show up."

"Lala, I'll be there."

"Ok, we'll see you tomorrow. Bye." As my call was wrapping up with Lala, Dior was beeping on the other line. I simply ignored it like I had been doing all her calls for the last few weeks. The crazy part was I really did want to speak with her but my life was on overload right now. Darnell used to handle a great deal of business for me and now that he was dead I had to oversee a lot of shit. I hadn't found anybody that was knowledgeable enough to maintain some of my important dealings that I also trusted. So the shit was all falling on me. And when my mind was consumed with business the last thing I could make time for was a woman like Dior. She took high maintenance to another level and I didn't mean simply materialistic wise, but emotional too. If I got on the phone with her she'd drill me about getting all her shit done and although I had every intention of coming through for her, right now it wasn't a priority for me. It wasn't even on my top five and I had no plans of talking to her until it was.

When I pulled up to my office building in Jersey City, I had this twinge of uneasiness. I wasn't sure if it was due to the edge not wearing off from the visit with my mother or something else. When I entered the building two of my security guards were in the lobby waiting for me. They nodded their head for me to go back outside so I made my exit and they followed behind me.

"What the fuck is going on?"

"We're not sure if the offices are secure."

"You think someone put a bug in the office?"

"We have our people up there checking now."

"So is that the situation?"

"That's part of it."

"What's the other part?"

"Alexus has been kidnapped and is being held for ransom."

"How much?"

"Two million."

"Who kidnapped Alexus and why do they think I would pay two million to get her back?"

"From my understanding this shit all goes back to Darnell. The money he was stealing from you, he wasn't giving it to anybody. He was keeping it for himself. The two guys he was partnering up with, he took their money too."

"So if he was stealing from all of us, where is all the money?"

"Nobody knows but them dudes want their money back and they somehow found out that Alexus wasn't Darnell's girl like they initially thought but that she actually worked for you."

"That's why you think the office might have a bug because they know this."

"Yes."

"How did they make contact?"

"It all went down right here."

"You talkin' 'bout today?"

"Yeah, right before I called you."

"Ok, Brice, I need you to take me through this shit step by step."

"Michael and Roy were upstairs. Me, Tony and Alexus was coming into the building. What looked like a delivery truck pulled up. Two guys came out in uniforms carrying boxes. By the time I realized something wasn't right they had pulled out guns and told us to get on the ground. They called us out by our names. Then a third guy came out the back of the truck and grabbed Alexus. He said Darnell stole their money and they wanted it back. He told us if we didn't give them two million the next time we saw Alexus she'd be floating in the Hudson River."

"Did you get the plate number?"

"Yeah, as soon as we heard them drive off we jumped up and got the information. I was tempted to start blazing on they ass but I knew they might end up killing Alexus and in this area, people hear gunshots they most def calling the police. I know we don't want them involved. "

"Nah, we definitely don't want that. So what did you come up with when you ran the plates?'"

"Nothing, they were bogus."

"I figured that. Damn," I huffed. "Even if I pay them cats, they might still kill Alexus. That foul nigga Darnell making problems for me even from the grave."

"So what do you want us to do?"

"Get the money together but something ain't adding up."

"What do you mean?"

"If Darnell had gotten that much money together, that shit ain't just lying around somewhere. Where the fuck is it? The average nigga can't just hide two million dollars unless they just making up an amount tryna pinch me."

"Lorenzo, we found three bugs," Roy informed me as soon as he came out the building.

"How the fuck did they get up in my office and have time to do that shit." I noticed Tony put his head down. "Tony something you need to say?"

"Last week I did allow a new cleaning crew to come in. I'm sorry. They told me the regular company had outsourced them because they needed a fill in. Everything seemed legitimate so I didn't second guess them. That had to be when they did it. Lorenzo, I'm so sorry."

"Thank fuckin' goodness we don't discuss no real business in that bitch 'cause the way you just opening doors to mutherfucka's the feds would be hauling all of us off to jail! Fuuuuck!" I screamed out ready to put a bullet in Tony's head for being so careless.

"Lorenzo, I...."

"Yo, don't say shit to me right now. All I want you to do," I said pointing towards Brice, "is get the money together and let me know when they contact you. When they do, inform them that you ain't giving them shit until you get Alexus back alive. Then you find out what the fuck happened to that money Darnell stole and how much he got from them. You also find out who Darnell had partnered up with because after they give us Alexus, we will find them, take my money back and kill 'em. Now all of you get the fuck out my face."

"Lorenzo, what are you doing here? I thought you weren't coming until tomorrow."

"Can I come in?"

"Of course, I'm sorry, come in." Lala moved out the way and I came inside. When I left my office I didn't feel like going home and I found myself driving around thinking. I no longer wanted to think so I decided to come over and see Tania.

"Where's Tania?"

"Upstairs getting ready for bed."

"Can I go see her?"

"Yes, she'll be happy to see you." I went upstairs and Tania was in her bed, under the covers watching The Princess and the Frog. I sat down beside her and her entire face lit up.

"Uncle Lorenzo, I missed you," she hugged me and said. When her arms wrapped around me it felt like healing power. Her innocence sent calmness through me that I needed. I knew it would and that's why I came. In my world, surrounded by hell right here on earth, having a child like Tania share the purity of her love was the only thing that saved me.

"I missed you too but now I'm here and I'm not leaving until you fall asleep."

"Then I'm never going to fall asleep because I don't want you to ever leave me."

"It's okay for you to go to sleep because I'll be back again."

"No you won't. You'll leave me like my daddy did and never come back."

"Tania, I put this on everything, I'll always come back for you."

"You promise?"

"I promise." She held on to me for dear life and I didn't let her go until she fell asleep in my arms. When I went downstairs Lala was sitting on the couch as if she'd been waiting for me.

"You were up there for a long time."

"Yeah, I wanted to stay until Tania went to sleep."

"That was sweet of you to do that."

"No, it was sweet of her to let me. I needed that time with her more than she probably needed it with me."

"What's going on with you?"

"Typical stress from work."

"There's nothing typical about your work, Lorenzo. Sit down. Let me get you something to drink."

"That would be good. And a shot of Hennessy would be even better."

"You're in luck." Lala came back out with a double shot of Hennessy and that shit went down my throat so smoothly.

"I needed that, thank you."

"Let me make you feel better, Lorenzo." Lala was on her knees in front of me. Her face was so angelic as if she had never been through pain but I knew that wasn't true.

"You've already made me feel better."

"Let me do more," she said unbuttoning my shirt.

"Don't do that," I said grasping her hands.

"Why won't you let me in?" I moved her hair from her face and glided my finger down her cheek.

"Because I have nothing to give."

"Well I do." Lala then pressed her lips against mine and the softness further relaxed me. I pulled her sweater over her head and my hands cupped her breasts as I let my tongue lick her hardened nipples. Lala's seductive moaning made my dick even harder.

"I want to be inside of you."

"I've always wanted that," Lala said in a breathless voice before taking off her jeans and panties. As she stood in front of me I let my hands gently caress the thickness of each curve before I laid her down on the couch. At that moment I was pleased I stayed prepared by always keeping condoms in my wallet because I was ready to go in when she spread her legs open as if begging to let me in. "Ahhhh," echoed through the room as I filled her insides and her wet juices coated my dick. Her pussy wasn't too wide or too tight, it was just right. As I went deeper and deeper and Lala's moans and groans of pleasure grew louder I knew since I went there, I could never turn my back on her.

Dior

All Of The Lights

⋆⋆★⋆⋆

"Hello," I answered in a real bad fuckin' mood. For one I was getting a pedicure that I couldn't afford and two I didn't recognize the number and I regretted even taking the call.

"Is this Dior?"

"Who wants to know?"

"This Quinton from King Magazine." I bit down on my bottom lip trying to gain my composure.

"Hey Quinton, what's up?" I asked trying to sound real non-pressed.

"Lorenzo gave me your number so we could connect on this magazine shoot."

"What shoot?"

"For the cover. Lorenzo didn't tell you?"

"Oh that's right. I've been so busy lately I almost forgot."

"I understand but do you think we can do this tomorrow?"

"Tomorrow coming up?"

"Yeah, I don't know another tomorrow. I know it's short notice but we want you for the issue coming up and we *real real* behind. We need to go to print like yesterday. It's my fault. I was supposed to get in touch with you a few weeks ago but I got caught up in some other things then I misplaced your number and had to call Lorenzo to get it again. So you think you can come through?"

"I guess I can make it happen," I said like my calendar was full when I didn't have shit on it.

"Cool, that's what's up. I'ma text you with the time and location information. I appreciate you doing this on such short notice."

"No problem."

"So I'll see you tomorrow but if you have any problems you can hit me back on this number, it's my cell."

"Will do, thanks." When I hung up the phone I wanted to jump up and do a fucking happy dance. I couldn't believe Lorenzo had really come through. I hadn't been able to get him on the phone in weeks and I was cussing his ass out every day. Now I felt kinda bad so I called him to let him know how grateful I was that he delivered. But when I dialed his number the shit rang like always and then went to voicemail. I just hung up.

I was not comprehending how a nigga could hook up some major shit for you but then ignore your ass like he didn't want to be bothered. Trying to figure out this mutherfuckin' shit was driving me crazy. I mean everybody had a motive for doing something but it was like whatever Lorenzo's was didn't include him talking to me. But I refused to let not being able to get him on the phone ruin my high.

I was about to call Brittani and share my news but scratched that. I was going to stick to the original plan. She would see the shit when it came out like everybody which would be soon. I was so damn happy I had been so broke because that meant I couldn't eat good. With no time to starve myself for the shoot I had already being doing that out of necessity. So tomorrow I would be cover girl ready without even trying.

When I hit the location early the next morning I was ready for them to get me prepared for my close-up. I sat in the chair and let the makeup artist beat my face until you couldn't see a trace of a blemish. They had a bitch looking so damn polished I wanted to fuck myself.

"For the cover shot we want you to wear the

same bra and panty set you wore on Phenomenon's video, since you know that's what put you on everybody's radar," the stylist informed me when she walked up.

"That's cool with me. Did they give it to you?"

"Oh yeah! That was the concept we always planned to go with so we requested it from the stylist that worked on the video weeks ago. The headline on the cover is going to be, 'Meet The New Phenomenon' you know a play on words but also incorporating the video."

"Whatever you wanna do, I'm ready."

"Great, we'll see you on the set in a few."

I was getting anxious waiting for the makeup artist to make his final touches. "What is your name? Because you are fierce with a brush."

"Cornelius aka Black Glamour."

"You have to make sure you give me your number before I leave. When I blow up I want you to be my personal makeup artist."

"No problem, doll," he said handing me his business card. I gladly took it and went in my dressing room to get ready. I slipped on the gray laced bra and panty set. I looked at myself in the mirror and I was feeling like a superstar although I wasn't one yet. Right when I was about to walk out I heard my cell ringing and it was Lorenzo.

"Damn, I can't believe you on the other end of my phone," I spit in a half joking, half serious voice.

"Don't start. I was checking to see if Quinton got in touch with you."

"We so pass the getting in touch phase. My makeup is done. I'm in my bra and panties about to hit the set."

"Right now?"

"Yep, it was some extra last minute shit but that always brings out the best results."

"I'm glad everything worked out."

"Me too. But seriously, Lorenzo, thank you for making this happen for me. I ain't gon' lie I was doubting you but you came through. I so needed this."

"If you ever get to know me Dior, you'll know I ain't gon' tell you nothing I can't deliver on."

"I'm learning quickly to not be a doubter when it comes to you."

"Good. Now go out there and give King the best cover they've ever seen."

"Wait," I called out so he wouldn't hang up the phone.

"What is it?"

"You have to come to New York so we can celebrate."

"I'm already in New York."

"That's even better. Maybe we can go out tonight or tomorrow. If I should celebrate with anybody it should be you."

"Thanks for the offer but I got too much

business to handle to celebrate anything. But you go out and have a good time. We'll celebrate in the next couple weeks once I've gotten my business under control."

"If that works best for you then that's what we'll do."

"Good, now go have some fun and don't blow it."

"You don't have to worry. I was born ready for this opportunity."

"I know you were, just wanted to hear you say it. Bye, Dior."

"Bye." I wasn't exaggerating when I said I was born ready for this. I had named it a long time ago and now it was time for me to claim it."

"Hey, Brittani," I said all extra cheerful on the phone. "I was just about to call you."

"To what, tell me you're on the cover of the next issue of King Magazine about to hit stands any day now."

"You heard about it already?" I asked in an excited voice.

"Yeah, all the blogs posted it."

"Perfect!"

"When did you shoot it, and why didn't you tell me?"

"Remember that thing I said I had brewing but I didn't want to mention it until it actually happened?"

"Clearly it happened and it must have been awhile ago if it's already about to drop."

"I only did it a few weeks ago, it was a rush job. I wanted to share the news when it was actually done and out."

"You so paranoid. They ain't gon' have you show up to shoot the damn thing only to shelve it."

"Listen, you never know how the cookies will crumble when you dealing with these industry types. I was waiting for everything to be on the up and up."

"Now you know, so you don't have to hold back. This really is a great look for you."

"I know! With all the bullshit I've been dealing with lately shit is finally coming together for me. I want you to come out tomorrow. They're having a party to celebrate my cover. It should be super cute."

"Wow! You getting the royal treatment."

"That's why I want you there so we can both overindulge."

"Say no more. This my type of shit. Now let me go so I can find an outfit for tomorrow."

"Awesome, you know you're more than welcome to raid my closet even though I'm not big on sharing but you're my bestie."

"Thanks for the offer, but come on now, you

ain't got no new hot shit I want to wear."

"Say that now, but give me a couple of months. You'll be dying to raid my closet and I'ma be like 'No Mam'."

"I'll take my chances."

"Remember you said that, but go 'head and tend to Destiny 'cause I hear her whining for you in the background." We both laughed. "I'll talk to you later."

When I got off the phone I went straight to my computer so I could see what people were saying about me on the blogs. The comments were relatively good but there were a couple of certified groupie haters posting bullshit comments. But that was ok with me because I knew it came with the territory when you put yourself out there.

After surfing through all the blogs, I put a call in to Lorenzo. Once again I hadn't spoken to him in ions but to my surprise he answered. "What's good, Lorenzo?"

"You tell me."

"Everything is going great. The magazine is actually throwing me a party tomorrow and I was hoping you could come. And don't tell me it's last minute so you can't make it because I sent you a text with all the details a few weeks ago."

"Yeah, I got it but I was extremely busy."

"So does that mean you are coming?"

"I'ma try my hardest. You know I wanna

support you."

"I need all the people who want me to win, there showing love."

"Listen, Dior, don't ever question if I want you to win because I do. When I don't answer my phone or call you back it's because I'm handling business. I got a lot going on and most of the time I just can't talk. But I will be at your party tomorrow night and we're going to celebrate. I will also be buying up every copy of the magazine I can get my hands on."

"Lorenzo, you're the best!"

"Hold up. I think we have a bad connection. Did you just say I was the best?"

"Stop with the bullshit," I laughed. "Yes, I think you are the best. I still don't know why you're doing so much for me but I really am grateful."

"You ever heard this old song by the group Wham, it's called Everything She Wants?"

"No! Who the hell is Wham?"

"It's a group George Michael started out in."

"I wouldn't peg you for listening to George Michael's music."

"I listen to all sorts of music. But when you get a chance check out that song, listen to the lyrics."

"Why?"

"Because it somewhat reminds me of you, especially the line 'Everything she wants is everything she sees' that's why I'm doing what I am for you."

"Because I want everything I see?"

"No, because you're bold enough to ask for it and not feel any shame for wanting it. I find that appealing." When Lorenzo said that I was tempted to be bold and ask him for some damn money. I knew he would give it to me but one thing I learned early on in playing the game of money and men. If a man thinks all you need is basic bullshit to be satisfied then that's all you'll ever get from him—and money for bills was basic shit, I don't care how much they added up to. I would just have to hang in there for a little while longer and be broke.

"Men have told me a lot of different reasons they find me appealing but that was never one of them."

"Never worry about what a man tells you, be concerned about what he doesn't tell you. I'll see you tomorrow night, Dior."

For a few minutes after Lorenzo hung up I stood there trying to analyze our entire conversation. He was very intriguing for several different reasons and I almost missed out on ever finding that out. When I met him at the club, I turned him down flat because I was too busy chasing after Sway. If he hadn't come to find me none of the things that were happening for me now would be. It was crazy; the person I didn't want to give two seconds of my time was the one who was giving me what I desired most.

"Yo, this party really is cute! They laid it out nice for you," Brittani beamed.

"Yeah, and mad celebrities showed up. These pics will be everywhere tomorrow."

"Hi Dior." A girl said, waving and walking up on me. "Remember me, I'm Courtney."

"Yes, hey Courtney." I quickly recognized her sweet face. "This is my friend, Brittani."

"Hi, it's nice to meet you," Courtney said, smiling at Brittani who was halfway paying attention. "Dior, you look absolutely gorgeous on your cover. I'm so proud of you," Courtney said, putting her attention back on me.

"You say the sweetest things to me, thank you."

"With that face and your body, you make it easy."

"Courtney, put your number in my phone. We have to stay in touch. You're fabulous for my ego."

"You're so funny, Dior."

"No, I'm so serious. I need a girl like you in my life."

"Sure, it would mean everything to me to be your friend."

"You keep saying all the right things we'll be friends forever. So enjoy the party and I will be in touch."

"I'll be waiting to hear from you, thanks again!" she said waving bye.

"Dior, stay away from that little girl."

"Why?"

"Because she really is sweet and she doesn't need to be corrupted by you."

"That's not funny, Brittani."

"I wasn't trying to be. We go way back. I got nothing but love for you but it's no secret how we get down, especially you. That little girl isn't ready and probably never will be, for what she would learn from you."

"Every time I run into her she makes me feel good. Everybody needs a person like that in their life. I'm glad I ran into her and I am going to call her. This night is turning out to be almost perfect."

"Why only almost? I can't think of nothing that would make it better."

"When Lorenzo gets here then it will be perfect."

"Lorenzo, who the hell is Lorenzo? I've never heard you mention that name before."

"He's the guy that made all this possible. He promised he would be here and surprisingly I'm disappointed that he hasn't shown up to share this night with me."

"Wow, so am I! I hope he does show up 'cause I can't wait to see this Lorenzo dude, especially since he got you waiting for his arrival...interesting."

"What's interesting is who just walked through the door, look." I pointed my finger towards the entrance and shook my head. "If he came to embarrass me I swear I'm leaving."

"Are you crazy, you can't leave your own party. Make his ass leave!"

"Brittani, as tempting as that sounds, let's not get it twisted. I'm on the cover of a booty magazine and that's Sway Stone. Who do you think they care more about?"

"I get your point, but you still can't let him run you out of your own party."

"You're right and I'm not. Come with me, I'ma go ask Phenomenon if he knows when Lorenzo is coming."

"So Phenomenon is cool with Lorenzo, is he the one that hooked you up with the video?"

"Pretty much."

"Now it's all making sense. So what does this Lorenzo guy do, is he in the music industry?"

"He definitely has dealings with the industry but I'm not sure exactly what he does. He seems to have his hands in a few things since he's always too busy handling business to talk to me."

"I see somebody has gotten under your skin. And I'm glad because anybody is better than Sway."

"Hey Phenomenon, have you talked to Lorenzo tonight?"

"Yeah, I spoke to him on my way here."

"Did he tell you what time he was coming?"

"Oh, he ain't gonna be able to make it. He got some other shit going on."

"Really, well that's cool," I said walking off feeling like I had just got stood up for the prom. This bizarre sense of devastation came over me and I didn't like it at all.

"Are you okay?"

"I'm fine Brittani," I snapped. "This is my night to shine, fuck Lorenzo! Let's go have some fun." I dragged Brittani to the middle of the dance floor. Kanye West's new song was playing and my body swayed to the music as I tried to escape thinking about Lorenzo and lose myself in my own world.

"I always loved the way you move," a voice that I was way too familiar with whispered in my ear. His hand held on tightly to my body as if it never stopped belonging to him.

"What do you want, Sway?" I asked turning around to face him.

"The same thing you want," he said, gripping under my chin firmly. He then took my hand and led me to his table without any resistance from me. I saw Brittani shaking her head in disapproval but I welcomed going back into Sway's world.

When we sat down, his bodyguards stood in front of our table, acting as a wall to shield us from everybody. "I know you've missed this," Sway said pulling out a vile of coke. And he was right. I hadn't snorted any coke since we were together. Sway always had access to the best quality of drugs which was a perk I lost when I wasn't with him. "Here," he said rubbing the white powder under my nose and over my lips. He then gripped the back of my hair tightly and put his tongue down my throat. As he eased up I began kissing him back.

After Sway dipped his finger in the coke I sniffed it off. He kept dipping and I kept sniffing. Before long he had my breasts out my dress licking each one, going back and forth and finger fucking me at the same time. While he did this I kept snorting coke as if making up for all the weeks I had been without it. I couldn't decide which one was bringing me the most pleasure, the foreplay or the coke play.

"Are you ready to feel this dick inside you?"

"Yes," I purred, ready to ride him right here in the booth.

"Then let's go."

"Can't you put it in right now?"

"What I have planned for you we can't do it in here. Now let's go."

I pulled my dress up and down and wiped off as much of the white stuff from my face as possible. But it didn't matter, Sway's bodyguards surrounded us so people could only catch slight glimpses as we made our exit to his awaiting car. During the ride back to his crib, we continued to snort coke and drink champagne. He even gave me a couple pills that I swallowed wanting to take my high as far as it could go.

"I want you to suck my dick," Sway demanded pulling down his pants. He took some of the coke and sprinkled it on his dick which had me crawling over to him quickly. "Yeeessss," Swayed groaned as my tongue teased his dick before my mouth took over.

By the time we reached Sway's penthouse my dress was practically off and I couldn't wait to fuck. But Sway had a different agenda. The moment the front door closed I was hitting the floor of the spacious mosaic marble foyer from the powerful impact of his backhand slap. "You didn't think I was going to take you back without punishing you first."

"Sway," I muttered, looking up to the glass chandelier that had water features. I had never really noticed that but while I tried to massage away the sting Sway left on my face I focused on it but not for long because he didn't let up. Sway tore off my dress before grabbing me by my hair. He lifted me up, dragging me across the floor like a rag doll into his bedroom. This certainly wasn't the first time Sway had put his hands on me but normally it would be one quick hit to remind me to stay in my place but this was different.

"I can't mess up that pretty face because

when the photogs take our pictures we don't want any obvious bruises now do we," Sway said with a sinister smile on his face. "But there are other ways to make sure you remember never to disrespect me again."

Sway tossed me down on his bed and walked over to his drawer and pulled out a long thick black belt. My first instant was to run out his place, butt ass naked and all but between the coke, champagne, pills and the initial slap I couldn't even muster enough strength to get up off the bed. The coke had my heart racing and head spinning. I assumed the pills were what had me unable to move. "Sway, don't do this," I mumbled.

"It's for your own good," he said before the first whip ripped across my butt. "If I could I would take this belt and whip your entire body. But I have some upcoming events we'll be attending," he paused mid sentence before lashing down three more whips, "and I'm not sure if your outfits are going to expose your back, legs and arms so to be safe I'll just whip yo' ass." I always knew Sway was crazy but this was taking it way too far.

"Baby, that's enough," I pleaded barely audible.

"You're right. I don't want to split any of your skin." And just that quickly Sway dropped the belt and took off his clothes. He got in the bed and the next thing I knew we were both sleeping.

When I woke up my ass was burning and my

mind started replaying the events of last night. "That nigga whipped me," I said out loud realizing that what happened wasn't some sort of bad nightmare but my reality. I looked around the bedroom but I didn't see Sway. I eyed the clock and couldn't believe it was the middle of the afternoon. I had basically slept the day away. Before I could try to get up I heard the bedroom door open.

"Mr. Stone has instructed me to run you a bath," some woman said walking past me.

"Who are you?"

"I'll be helping you get prepared for the event you'll be attending with Mr. Stone."

A few minutes after the woman went in the bathroom Sway came in. "Drink this protein shake and take this pill," he directed as if he hadn't just beat me with a belt last night. "We have a lot to do tonight so I need you to get your energy up."

"I'm not going anywhere with you tonight."

"Yes you are, now take this."

"Sway my ass is still hurting from what you did to me."

"This pill, the drink and bath, all of that will make you feel better."

"Give it to me." I gulped down the pill with the protein shake which was actually very tasty. "So where are we going tonight?"

"I'm headlining a charity event."

"Are you performing?"

"No, they didn't have enough money for me to perform too. Some other artist are performing, I'm only hosting. Let me see your face, I want to make sure I didn't leave a bruise from the slap yesterday." He held my chin up looking to see what damage if any he caused. "There's a slight mark but nothing some makeup can't cover up."

"You shouldn't have hit me in the first fuckin' place."

"I can't wait to fuck you later on. I know you can't get on your back right now because you're sore. But you'll be good by tonight," he told me, totally ignoring what I had just said.

"I don't know why I keep fuckin' with you."

"Yes you do, because you love being with a Superstar and you hope some of it will rub off on you. You got your little King Magazine cover but you know nothing is going to bring you the type of attention you crave like being with me."

"I don't even like you. You make me sick!"

"No you make yourself sick. I'm 'bout to start shooting my video for the lead single off my new CD. I want you for the lead."

"Why? I thought you had no interest in giving me shine."

"You did Phenomenon's video and now you're on the cover of King with that bullshit headline. So people won't start giving him credit for blowing you up, I want you in my video. I need everybody to know you're my project."

"Now I'm your project how convenient."

"You need to be thanking me. After being in my world I know it had to be depressing to go back to yours. But now we have a better understanding. I'll let you shine just make sure you follow my rules."

"Mr. Stone, her bath is ready."

"You heard the lady, go 'head. I'll be back shortly."

"Since you're talking about rules I have one of my own."

"What's that?"

"I don't want Tracy or Lori in my presence. If you want to still fuck them go 'head but not around me and that's nonnegotiable."

"Not a problem but don't develop a habit of making rules because most of them won't apply to me but remember, all of my rules apply to you." I watched as Sway left the room before I got up.

When I stepped in the whirlpool I looked around the Italian marble bathroom with mother of pearl inlays and the rainforest Swiss steam shower. It was a stark contrast to the bathroom I had in my New York City apartment. Yeah, Sway was right there was no comparison to what it was like being in his world. His fame provided him with a lifestyle that only a handful of people ever got to experience and I was one of them. If only I could come up with a way to be able to get it for myself. I really started to believe that Lorenzo would make that possible for me but he didn't even show up to my party. It was like I started off as some sort of game for him and somewhere down the line he got bored and decided to toss me to the side. Sway seemed to be my only hope but the price was so high when it came to dealing with him. I would make it work though and having plenty of drugs to keep me medicated would make it that much easier. In the serenity of the hot water, I closed my eyes and let my mind drift away.

Lorenzo

Blame Game

★ ⋆★⋆★⋆ ★

"How was the party?" I asked, after placing my order with the waitress. I had been ripping and running so hard in the last forty-eight hours that I wasn't even eating. So when Phenomenon called to meet for lunch, I welcomed the break and an opportunity to eat a good meal.

"It was cool. It was a nice turnout. I met me a cutie and got plenty of shine. I guess that's what it's all about. Oh, and I think you broke homegirl's heart. Even though she tried to play if off I could tell Dior was disappointed you didn't come through."

"Why you say that?"

"'Cause she asked me where you were and when I told her you wasn't gonna' be able to make it, her face damn near cracked. I had no idea you was kickin' it wit' her."

"We're not. I'm just helping her out with some things."

"That's cool, I think she back wit' Sway anyway."

"Back with Sway, when did that happen?"

"He came to her party. I didn't see them together but they're in today's paper. She went with him to some charity event last night."

"Yo, she's crazy."

"That's what being in this industry will do to you, make you crazy. I'm finding myself already giving into it. What they say, fame is more addictive than heroin." As Phenomenon rambled on about the pitfalls of being in the entertainment industry my mind wandered to Dior. She had called me a couple times the night of the party but I couldn't answer my phone. Dealing with Alexus kidnapping and other bullshit, there was no way I could break free and deal with a bunch of phony mutherfuckers at a party. But I should've never told Dior I was coming and have her find out I wasn't from Phenomenon. Now she was back with Sway. I decided to call her since I was in the city.

"I'll be right back." I got up from the table and stepped outside to call Dior.

"Hey Lorenzo, it was great seeing you at my

party the other night. Oh, that's right you didn't show up." The fact that Dior greeted me with so much sarcasm let me know Phenomenon was right. It really did bother her that I didn't come to her party.

"I apologize, Dior, but..."

"Save it! I've never had one man give me so many excuses in all my life. If you don't want to be bothered with me then just say that and stop playing these games."

"Can I see you?"

"You want me to tell you yes so you can have me standing around looking stupid—forget it."

"I'm in the city right now and I want to see you."

"Seriously?"

"Yes, can I?"

"Yes. I'm at home. I'll be here for the next couple of hours. You can come by."

"Okay, text me your address. I'll be there in an hour."

"Are you really coming, Lorenzo?"

"Yes, I promise I'll be there."

"Ok."

When I got back to the table the waitress was bringing our food. "Everything cool?" Phenomenon questioned when I sat down.

"Yeah, I just have to see somebody before I leave the city."

"I got you. I know you a busy man but don't

forget my album release party is in a few weeks."

"That's right. It's finally dropping. Where you having it at?"

"In this penthouse suite at a hotel in Midtown. It's gon' be private and intimate but still off the chain."

"That's cool. I'll be there." I had some more small talk with Phenomenon and finished up my food before heading out. I had a slew of shit to handle and really didn't have time to see Dior. But something told me if I didn't go see her today then our chances of ever getting together were done.

When I got to her apartment building the doorman let me in. I then waited for the concierge to call and let her know I was here. During my ride up on the elevator I thought about what I was trying to accomplish by coming over here. I didn't know if I wanted to fit Dior into my life on a part-time or full-time basis. That's why I hated making spontaneous moves but under the circumstances I didn't have a choice, because there was one thing I was sure of—I wanted her. When I reached her door I knocked. I could hear music playing and then she opened the door. I wasn't greeted with the makeup and over-the-top glamour I was used to seeing from her but in her tank top, boy shorts and disheveled hair she looked more beautiful to me than she ever had before. I didn't even let Dior speak. I stepped forward and began kissing her. It lasted for what seemed like forever and I just stopped suddenly. I looked down at her because without the super high heels she was rather petite. Her eyes, the way she stared at me was turning me on something crazy so I started kissing her again. This time she stopped but only to shut the door.

We went back to kissing and I peeled off her tank top and shorts. I lifted her up and carried her into her bedroom. After I laid her down, I carefully studied her body and she was so fuckin' sexy it just made me want to taste her so I did. My tongue got completely lost in her juices. Her nails pressed deeply into my back as my tongue continued to gently massage her clit. She wrapped her legs around me and began rubbing her breasts and playing with her own nipples as her pussy fucked my mouth. She was a woman that was created to strictly pleasure men and that had to be a gift and a curse.

When I finally put my dick inside of her, I started off slow and gentle but soon each thrust became more meaningful. Dior's cries of pleasure and pain had me lost inside of her. The warmth and wetness of her pussy had my dick hypnotized. Our mouths reconnected and her kisses were so passionate it made me press so deep that I thought my dick was going to reach her throat. I couldn't get enough of her. It seemed like we had been making love forever. I wanted to pull out but I couldn't stop. Before I knew it I was emptying myself inside of her. So not only did I not wear a condom which was supposed to be an essential, I was cumming inside her.

"Lorenzo, I love you."

"I love you too." Right after the words left my mouth I couldn't believe I said it. Besides my mother I never told a woman I loved them before and there was no way I could love Dior or did I. I lifted my body off of her and laid on my back, closing my eyes wondering how we got to this moment of exchanging words like I love you.

"I'm not on the pill, what if I got pregnant. Would you want to have a baby with me?"

"No."

"That's cold." I opened my eyes and looked at her.

"You don't want a baby, Dior."

"Don't put this off on me. I asked you a question and you answered it." She turned away from me with a hurt expression on her face. I kissed her neck and kept kissing until I worked my way down to her breasts. Her nipples were hard again and so was my dick so I found myself going right back inside of her. Her pussy was still warm and wet. Just like before I had no self control and couldn't pull out. I came inside of her again and this time I just laid there.

"If I get pregnant, I'ma have it." I couldn't believe this woman that had nothing maternal about her was talking about having my baby like we'd been together forever. But then I couldn't believe I kept cumming inside of her like I wanted to make a baby with her.

"No you're not."

"I told you I'm not on the pill. Why did you cum inside me again if you don't want to get me pregnant?"

"I don't know I'm confused by that shit too. But it's not you. I don't want to have a baby period."

"Never?"

"Never!"

"I thought all men wanted at least one child."

"Not this man."

"Why not?"

"If you really want to know, my mother is schizophrenia and I don't want to take a chance of having a child born with it."

"I'm sorry about your mother but just because she has it doesn't mean your child will too."

"It's hereditary and it's a very good chance my child could. I wouldn't want them to have to live with something like that."

"So just say you got me pregnant today you would want me to have an abortion?"

"You're not pregnant. What is up with you and all this baby talk?"

"When I said I loved you I meant it, did you?"

"When I said it, yeah I did mean it but do I really love you. I don't know, Dior. I feel something for you and it's different than anything I ever felt before but love..." my voice trailed off because I wasn't sure what was going on with me.

"Fine, I guess we'll just go back to how things were."

"You know we can't do that."

"It's like every since I initially turned you down you've been playing a game with me. But you win because I've caught real feelings for you and you don't want me. So I'ma stick to what I know."

"And what's that being Sway's personal whore? I know you're back together with him."

"So is that what this was all about. Since you know I'm back with Sway you wanted to see if you could get me to fuck you?"

"No. I don't know why I came over here. I want you. I've always wanted you but my life is complicated."

"You're not making any sense. If you want me then why not be with me?"

"You're so caught up in Sway's world and this fame bullshit. You act like you can commit to me and be my woman."

"I can. You've already proven you can help me obtain the fame I want. You can keep doing it. But instead of doing it as a favor we can do it as a couple."

"Dior, as much as I want you, you require too much work. I don't have the time to invest in you like that. I'll keep helping you as much as I can with your career but being a couple isn't possible." Her eyes watered up and I felt an ache in my heart that I hurt her with my words. But I never learned how to be anything but honest.

"I understand," she said wiping away a single tear that rolled down her cheek. "I guess you better go. I need to finish getting my things together."

"Where are you going?"

"I'ma start back staying with Sway."

"You don't have to do that, Dior. I can provide you with everything you want. You don't have to be with Sway to live a good life."

"So you'll provide for me but I'm not good enough to be your woman."

"That's not what I said, Dior."

"Damn if it isn't! At least I know what it is with Sway but you'll have my heart and at the same time remind me that I'll never have yours. So no thanks to your kept woman offer."

"So you're going back to Sway?"

"Isn't that where a loser woman like me is supposed to be."

"Would you stop with that dramatic bullshit," I said, picking up my cell phone seeing the shit load of missed calls I had. "Listen, I have to go we'll continue this conversation later."

"Does later mean tonight, tomorrow, next week or next month? I just wanted an idea so I would know how long I should wait because I know how busy you are."

"I'll call you tonight. And don't make any decision about staying with Sway until after we talk."

"I won't but you better call me tonight, Lorenzo."

"I will," I said putting my clothes on. "Wait for me." I kissed Dior on her lips and left.

Dior

Lost In The World

★·★·★·★·★

"Dior, thank you again for getting me on this video. I can't believe I'm in a Sway Stone video," Courtney gushed as we waited in my dressing room for the next scene.

"When Sway said they needed a girl to play an angel, you were the first person to come to mind."

"My friends still don't believe me. Wait till they see the video! But my part doesn't compare to yours, you're the leading lady as you should be. How is it being Sway's girlfriend on the video and in real life, it's got to be so cool."

"It's everything you can imagine and more," I answered before snorting a line of coke. When I looked up I saw Courtney staring at me with her mouth wide open. "I'm assuming you don't snort coke," I laughed trying to make her feel at ease.

"No," she said, shaking her head. "I don't do any drugs or even drink for that matter."

"That's really good, Courtney. Stay that way. Drugs are very bad for you."

"Then why do you do them?" I looked at her strangely because nobody had ever asked me that question. That was probably because most of the time I was using drugs so was everybody else around me.

"When I'm high I don't have to think about anything. I just live my life." Courtney shook her head as if she didn't understand what I meant but how could she, she didn't do drugs.

"Open the fuckin' door," I heard Sway scream.

"Courtney, will you open the door for him?"

"Sure!"

"What the fuck are you doing in here? You supposed to be on set," Sway barked, rudely brushing past Courtney as if he didn't even see her. But Courtney's star gazing made her oblivious to it.

"Nobody told me so I didn't know."

"You're fuckin' high that's why you didn't know," Sway said putting his tongue down my throat.

"Stop," I said, pushing him away. "I'm not high. I only did two lines.

"Don't tell me to stop." Sway held my hair tightly

and started kissing me again.

"We have company, can't we do this later."

"You talkin' 'bout her," he nodded towards Courtney as if he just realized she was in the room with us.

"Yes, who else would I be talking about?"

"She's cute. What's her name?"

"Why don't you ask her yourself? She's standing right there."

"What's your name?"

"Courtney. I'm playing the angel."

"What the fuck, an angel?"

"For the video Sway, your video," I rolled my eyes.

"Oh, so you partying with us tonight?"

"Cool! Party with Sway Stone...yes!"

"Sway, she's not that type."

"She just said she wanted to party with us."

"Her partying and our partying are different."

"Then maybe we need to break her in. She seems ready to me."

"Courtney, can you excuse us for a second?"

"Sure, Dior. I'm going to get a soda, do you want me to bring you anything back?"

"No, I'm good, just close the door behind you... thanks."

"Stay away from her, Sway. She's not like the rest of these little whores you fuck and toss to the side."

"Are you being protective over somebody? That's epic. And I thought the only person you gave a fuck about was yourself."

"Whatever, but Courtney is off limits."

"Fine, all I said was I thought she was cute but you're my baby."

"Would you stop with all this kissin'."

"What the fuck is wrong wit' you? You been prancin' 'round here wit' a bad attitude for the last couple of weeks."

"I'm fine, I'm just tired."

"I know what it is, my baby needs a vacation. We wrap up the video today. Later in the week let's go to Cabo for a few days."

"Sounds good. Now let me freshen up so I can get on the set."

"A'ight, see you in a few." When Sway left I glanced up and caught my reflection in the mirror. Each curl was falling just right and my makeup was highlighting my best features perfectly. I looked like I had it all. Since my party and getting back with Sway I had been a fixture on the blogs daily and in all the weekly tabloids. I had even got a couple offers for a possible reality show and some guest spots on television shows but the one thing I hadn't received was that phone call from Lorenzo. Everybody seemed to want me but him and it was totally sending me to the breaking point. I had left so many messages begging him to reach out to me but they all went ignored. That day he walked out my apartment he knew he wasn't coming back for me, he just got some sick pleasure out of emotionally torturing me. The only thing that had got me through the pain of his rejection was drugs but it still didn't get him completely out of my mind.

"Dior, they're waiting for you," I heard Courtney say in the background interrupting my mental pity party.

"Coming," I said, before sniffing one more line and wiping the left over powder from my nose.

When we arrived at the penthouse suite on the 53rd floor, I was impressed with the spot Phenomenon chose to have his album release party at. I had never been to this hotel and it was gorgeous. It was two huge floors that connected by a dramatic staircase and the color tones were like silvery, midnight blues, metallic and gold's. And the views were fucking incredible. There were bay windows on three sides with views of Central Park, the Hudson River, George Washington Bridge and the stunning Manhattan skyline. Then there was this, what looked to be a 13 or 14-foot curved sofa in leather and velvet in the center of the room.

"I might need to have my next party here,"

Sway commented also impressed with the spot. I was surprised he even wanted to come but this was the party to be at tonight so of course Sway had to show his face.

"Yeah, it's incredible," I said, as we walked past the gas fireplace adorned with marble. The layout was so open that there were some people sitting at the expansive dining table, others were by the wet bar and then there was what had to be a specially designed rotating swivel 6-foot day-bed located in front of one of the bay windows. You could spin yourself to any view you pleased.

"What's up, Dior," Phenomenon said, giving me a hug. He nodded at Sway as if he didn't want to speak.

"Hey, congratulations. I know you're gonna move a lot of units."

"That's what they predicting. Pretty soon I'll be taking your spot, Sway."

"You got a long way before you get there. We talking millions, millions and millions of records. In my genre ain't nobody moving those type of numbers but me."

"All we can do is try," Phenomenon grinned. "You guys enjoy the party, oh and if you hungry, there's a full service kitchen at your disposal. The chef will cook whatever you like."

"Cool, thanks," I smiled. "Wow, I can't believe his label dropped this type of paper on his album release party."

"Please, these labels ain't spending that kind of money on new artist like Phenomenon or mostly any artist for that matter."

"Then who footing the bill, 'cause this shit definitely ain't no on a budget party."

"From what I understand Phenomenon has some major Drug Lord with an endless cash flow funding his project."

"Really, do you know him?"

"Maybe, maybe not. If I met him, I doubt he was advertising what he do. But I heard he's a real low key dude that stays in the background."

"There's Brittani over there by the bar, I'ma go speak."

"Go 'head I'll be over there in a minute."

It was nice to get away from Sway even if it was only for a brief period of time. I hurried over to Brittani. She greeted me with a warm smile which was nice since she had been pissed with me ever since I got back with Sway.

"Hey! It's good to see you."

"It's good to see you too. I didn't expect Sway to come to this party."

"I know but he has to be in the spotlight and this is where everybody is tonight."

"So what have you been up to? Every time I turn around you're being photographed or featured in something. I even read somewhere you're getting your own reality show. Is that true?"

"I've had a couple of offers but I haven't decided on anything yet."

"Do you even know what the show would be about?"

"Nope."

"Amazing, these networks are just throwing reality shows at anybody these days."

"Well tell me what you really think, Brittani."

"I wasn't trying to offend you. I'm just saying, one minute you're a nobody and then you do a video, a men's magazine and run around with the biggest narcissist of them all, Sway and all of sudden your face is everywhere and you're being offered a reality show. I'm officially putting you in the famous for what category."

"I don't need to hear this shit from you, Brittani."

"You need to hear it from somebody because I'm sure all the ass kissers you have surrounding you aren't telling you a damn thing."

"Are you jealous? Is that what this is about?"

"Jealous of what? All you do is party."

"You seem to be at the same party as me. Plus I know you and Kevin aren't together anymore. He's running around with that R&B singer. Is that what has you acting like your PMSing?"

"Don't concern yourself over my relationship with Kevin."

"Trust me, I'm not. All I'm trying to do is figure

out where all this negativity is coming from."

"You don't even see what you're becoming, Dior."

"What a star. I thought that's what we both wanted for me."

"If being with Sway is part of that stardom I'm not cosigning on it. He is poison and I'm starting to think you are too."

"I always thought I was the bitch out of the two of us...actually I am—you're just bitter. And good luck with Kevin. I hope those checks keep clearing," I said, walking away from Brittani and right into Lorenzo. "Excuse me. I didn't see you."

"I know but I saw you. You seemed to be in an intense conversation. I was waiting for you to finish. Can we go upstairs and talk?"

"I don't think that's a good idea. I'm here with Sway and he wouldn't be thrilled if he came looking for me and I was with you."

"Please, I really do need to talk to you."

"My cell works great. Is there a reason you haven't used that to talk to me in the last few weeks? Or is it just more convenient for you to talk to me here, since we're both at this party?"

"I know you're angry with me, and I don't blame you but just come with me so we can talk."

"I'm done talking to you. I have to go, Sway is waiting for me." As I walked towards Sway I could feel Lorenzo's eyes fixated on every step I made and

I planned to give him something to really be mad at.

"Who was that guy you were talking to?" Sway asked me when I reached him.

"Nobody."

"If he's nobody why is he staring at you like that?"

"Like what?"

"Like he's fucking you!"

"Baby, the only person who is fuckin' me is you. You know this pussy is all yours."

"You always know how to make my dick hard." Sway seized my ass and started kissing me right in the middle of the floor in front of everybody. I knew he would if I said that to him. It didn't take much for me to turn him on and once I did he couldn't control himself. I knew we were giving Lorenzo an eyeful and I relished in knowing that.

"Baby, don't you want to go fuck," I whispered in his ear between kisses.

"Oh yes," he moaned pulling me closer. He was damn near trying to fuck me right here on the floor.

"That's enough!" I heard Lorenzo say grabbing my arm. My eyes widened in shock. I knew he would be pissed by what I was doing but I didn't think he would call me on it in front of everybody. "You're coming with me, so we can talk, now!"

"Who the fuck is you? And get your hands off my girl!" Sway knocked Lorenzo's hand off my arm and Sway's security guards came running up to make sure he was protected. But then like six big bodyguards dressed in black seemed to come out of nowhere to protect Lorenzo. All I could do was wonder what the hell he did that warranted that sort of protection. Before any more words were exchanged massive chaos broke out between both sides of security. In the midst of that Sway grabbed my arm, pulling me out the suite and into the elevator.

"What the fuck just happened in there?" Sway yelled so loudly I thought my head would explode. "Answer me," he continued slamming me against the elevator door.

"I don't know!" I yelled back.

"Are you fuckin' that nigga? Why else would he grab on you like that!" As we were going down and the elevator stopped on another floor, when the doors opened he roared, "Step the fuck back, this elevator is out of order." The older couple ran back, startled and scared.

"Sway, would you stop it!"

"Shut the fuck up! Don't tell me what to do," he spit before hitting me in my face. By the time the elevator hit the bottom floor Sway was in full blown anger mode. He was using me as his personal punching bag. It was like a switch had gone off and he couldn't turn it back on. When the elevator doors opened I was crawling out and my face was battered, bruised and bloody. There was hotel security already in the lobby and the police were coming in. Between the old couple and the ruckus going on at the penthouse suite I wasn't surprised to see both but Sway was. He was totally shocked when the handcuffs clinched his wrist and he was arrested. I was taken to the hospital and all I thought about was that I hoped nobody got a picture of me looking like this.

"Courtney, thank you so much for coming over and bringing me something to eat."

"Of course, I would do anything for you, Dior."

"Is it still crazy out there?"

"Yes, it's like a zoo. There are photographers and news people everywhere. They all want to get a picture of your bruised face."

"It looks bad, doesn't it?" I could tell she didn't want to admit it, but Courtney nodded her head yes. But I didn't need her to tell me, I could look in the mirror and see the damage Sway did to me.

"I can't believe Sway beat you up like that. I would've never thought he was that type of guy. You know what happened has been on the news all morning and every radio station is talking about it."

"I know. The crazy part is that I always dreamed about getting publicity of this magnitude but I didn't want it like this. I don't even know what to say. They keep calling my phone, I can't leave my apartment. I just want it to stop."

"It's not going to stop anytime soon. Sway is an international superstar. He makes Chris Brown seem like a nobody and you know how long the media kept that story going. He has to be somewhere regretting he ever put his hands on you."

"Do you know if he's out on bail yet?"

"I'm sure he is. You know he has the best attorneys on speed dial. I can't imagine them letting him stay in jail."

"That's true but I figured if he was out he would've called me by now."

"You think he would have the audacity to call you after what he did!"

"Courtney, this isn't the first time Sway has put his hands on me. This is just the first time he got caught."

"If this is the life of the rich and famous I don't want any parts of it. I idolized Sway now you're telling me he's a typical woman beater." Courtney kept shaking her head as in disbelief.

"Courtney, don't idolize Sway or any of these people in the entertainment industry because they'll disappoint you every time."

I picked up the paper I had Courtney bring over and there was a picture from an event Sway and I attended together a few weeks ago splashed across the front page. If you went by the image of us we appeared to be the perfect couple. I was even smiling in the pic which was a joke in itself since Sway never made me smile. I didn't know how I could turn something so tragic into a positive. I was lost and I desperately needed some direction.

Complicated

★ ⋆ ★ ⋆ ★ ⋆

When I pulled up to Alexus's townhouse, I had so much shit on my mind, mainly Dior, that I was tempted to turn around. But she had been back home for over a week and this would be the first time I came to visit. Before I went inside I decided to try and call Dior again. Right when I was about to hang up she answered.

"Hi."

"I've been blowing your phone up, why haven't you answered?"

"I wasn't in the mood to talk."

"Now you are?"

"Not really. But I know how it feels to be ignored so I didn't want to keep doing it to you."

"I deserved that."

"What do you want, Lorenzo?"

"I want to know how you doing. I heard what Sway did to you after the party and I'm worried about you."

"Not good."

"I feel responsible for what happened. I know coming up to you like I did pissed him off. I had no idea he would lose it like that though."

"You're not responsible for Sway's behavior. Trust me, he had problems keeping his hands to himself before any of this went down."

"So that nigga had been puttin' his hands on you on a regular? Is that what you tellin' me?" I knew Dior could hear my anger building up and she didn't need that.

"No, that's not what I'm telling you," I felt she was lying but didn't want to push her.

"Then what are you saying?"

"I'm saying that whatever went down between me and Sway you're not responsible for it. So if that's all you called to tell me I'ma let you go."

"That's not the only reason I called."

"What else?"

"I want us to give this relationship thing a try."

"When did you decide that?"

"I've been thinking about it for awhile but I

didn't want to put it out there until I was a hundred percent sure that's what I wanted to do."

"And now you are sure?"

"Yes. Dior, I'm a complicated man which means I have a complicated life. It's hard for me to let people into my circle especially a woman. But I rather try with you than lose you."

"I want to say yes, let's do this but my life is so fucked up right now. I don't want to put you in the middle of all this pandemonium."

"I can handle it and so can you. The first thing we'll do is get somebody to straighten this mess out."

"How and who?"

"I'll hire the best public relations firm money can buy and they'll come up with a crisis management plan that will make all this bullshit work in your favor."

"You make it sound so simple."

"Money gives you options and the more options you have the more simple shit gets. Trust me, Dior, I got you."

"No more games?"

"No more games. When I make my mind up about something I see it all the way through. I've made up my mind that I want to be with you."

"I want that."

"Then that's what you'll have. I'ma come see you later after I handle things."

"I don't know if that's a good idea?"

"Why not?"

"The paparazzi are holding court in front of my building."

"It's that bad?"

"It's worse than bad. I didn't have anything to eat in here so I had a friend bring me over some food and some other stuff I needed. I can't leave my building."

"We'll figure it out but I need to be with you."

"I need to be with you too. I feel so alone."

"But you're not. I'm here for you no matter what."

"I love you, Lorenzo."

"I love you too. I'll see you tonight."

"Ok."

A sense of relief came over me when I got off the phone with Dior. I had been debating the decision I would make about where to go with our relationship up until the very moment I got her on the phone. It wasn't easy for me because there were certain aspects of my life I would have to open up to her about, if I let her into my world on a personal level. But last night the fury that overcame me when I saw her at that party with Sway established to me that without a doubt she was the woman I wanted to be with.

Now that I came to my decision I needed to get the rest of my life in order, starting with Alexus. When I rang the doorbell I heard the dog barking and a few seconds later Alexus came to the door.

"Lorenzo, what did I do to deserve a personal visit from you? I've been home for a little over a week. I was beginning to think you were never coming."

"You knew I was coming. Things have been out of my control lately but I came to see you the first chance I got." I gave Alexus a hug and we went to sit down in her living room. "It's got to feel good to be back home."

"It does. I know I told you over the phone but thank you for paying the ransom. When I heard the amount they were asking for I wasn't sure if you would think I was worth paying that much for." She gave a half-hearted laugh as if she was joking but I knew she was serious.

"Of course I was gonna pay it, no matter what the amount. But I was surprised they thought to make it that high. I mean how many people know I have access to that amount of cash."

"That's true but I guess desperate people do desperate things."

"Where is Deon?"

"Still visiting with my mother."

"It's a good thing he was in North Carolina when the kidnapping went down because getting him down there might've been difficult."

"Yeah, speaking of kids how is Tania doing?"

"She's good."

"You seem to be spending a lot of time with

her and Lala."

"Why do you say that?"

"A couple times I talked to you when I got back you were either on your way or had just left from being over there."

"I want to make sure they're good."

"I think that's noble, especially under the circumstances but be careful."

"Why do I need to be careful?"

"I know you Lorenzo and I hope you don't cross the line when it comes to Lala. I care about you and I would hate for you to make a mistake like that."

"I appreciate your concern but I got everything under control."

"I don't doubt that for a second. But like I said, I care about you and only want what's best for you."

"Thank you," I said, not convinced that was how Alexus really felt. The main reason it had taken me so long to visit her was because I still wasn't sure if she was friend or foe which was disturbing since she had been one of the few individuals I felt I could trust. My people were meticulously investigating how the whole kidnapping went down, not leaving nothing or no one off the hook. Alexus was at the top of my list although I hoped she hadn't committed the ultimate betrayal like Darnell had. So far everything was coming up clean on her but something didn't feel right. Normally, to put my mind at rest I would've had her killed just for thinking she was somehow involved but because she had a very young son, I held back. I wouldn't want to leave a child motherless unless I had no other choice. I prayed for his sake that she wasn't involved.

"Not to get off the subject but did you hear what happened at that artist's party you do some work with?"

"Yeah," I said, not letting her know I was dead in the center of it.

"It's a damn shame people who got everything going for them can't pull it together long enough to stay out of trouble. I mean look at this shit." Alexus held the front of the New York Post up. "Sway Stone who got all of hip hop and even pop on lock is in jail for beatin' some chick's ass."

"Let me see that." Alexus handed me the paper and I tried to read it without it appearing that I had a personal investment in the situation.

"I have to make sure I call Phenomenon to see if everybody involved is okay."

"They all okay I'm sure. The only one probably hurting right now is Sway. He got caught red-handed beating up on that girl. I don't see how he'll be able to get out of this. That is what I would define as a sticky situation."

I had no idea that Sway went off on Dior to that degree until after reading the article in the paper. Now I understood why she was on the brink of having a nervous breakdown. This shit ran much deeper than I initially thought. I couldn't waste any time finding a public relations firm to get to spinning. Unless Dior was ready to be the poster child for domestic violence this mess had to be cleaned up. I was positive Sway and his dream team machine were coming up with a creative list of actions to take to correct any damage currently done and bring a halt to what might be coming up. It didn't take a genius to figure out that step one would be to shut Dior down. So I had to set Dior's plan in motion before Sway had an opportunity to jumpstart his own.

By the time I left Alexus's house and arrived at Lala's place, I had been on the phone with a few PR firms that all came highly recommended. I wanted to personally speak with the person who would spearhead the project because I had to make sure they knew what the fuck they were doing. They needed to hear in my voice that I wasn't interested in them just talking a good game I wanted results. Also, with Sway being such a high profile celebrity I knew they would all be trying to jump on it so I had to be extra cautious. I narrowed my decision down to two firms that had equally impressed me. Once I received their written proposal that would determine my final decision.

When I got to Lala's front door Tania was right there ready to greet me, "Hi, Uncle Lorenzo!" I lifted her up and she gave me a hug and kiss. Tania had quickly turned into the daughter I would never have. Being a father had always been something I wanted but having to deal with the pain of my mother's mental disorder changed that. So having a Goddaughter like Tania was a blessing for me.

"How's my favorite girl doing?"

"Great! I'm drawing you a picture. I can't wait to show it to you."

"I can't wait to see it. Go get it."

"There are a couple more things I have to do to it, so stay right here. I'm going to finish and I'll be right back."

"You do that. I'll be right here waiting." Tania ran upstairs and all I could do was smile. I started to think about Dior and when she said she wanted us to have a baby.

"That little girl is something else."

"She is and she absolutely adores you, Lorenzo."

"I adore her too."

"And don't forget about her mother," Lala said, giving me a kiss. "My mother will be over here shortly to pick up Tania so we can have some private time. I can't wait to feel you inside me."

I had been intimate with Lala a few more times since the first time we had sex but my intention was to stop. I didn't want to hurt her. She just wasn't some woman I was fucking. I cared about her and I knew I didn't want anything serious. Now that I was going to try and make it work with Dior I knew it would be a huge mistake to keep sexing Lala.

"Listen, Lala, I bought a house for you and Tania."

"What! When did you do that and why?"

"I bought it recently. This neighborhood is cool but Tania's getting older, she deserves a big backyard, a pool, you know all the stuff that little kids enjoy."

"The house has a pool! Lorenzo, you are too good to us! It seems like a pretty big house. Why don't you move in with us?"

"That's the thing, Lala. I don't think we need to continue on with that type of relationship."

"I don't understand. I thought things were going great between us."

"They were but I don't wanna lead you on. Nothing more is gon' come outta this. You deserve to eventually find that man who wants to take it to the next level with you."

"And what you telling me is that it's not going to be you."

"Exactly."

"So why buy us the house, Lorenzo. To ease your guilt 'cause you don't want to fuck wit' me no more?"

"That's part of it. You're a good woman and Tania is my Goddaughter. I'll always take care of her and you. I want both of you to have a better quality of life and since I can provide it why not."

"A house is not going to replace my relationship with you, Lorenzo."

"Maybe not but living good will at least make you feel a little better."

"Are you still going to come visit Tania?"

"Of course and that's why I'm ending this thing between us. I don't want our relationship to jeopardize the relationship I have with Tania. I'm not gon' call what we were doing a mistake but we were both going through a difficult time and got caught up."

"Maybe that's what it was for you but not for me. I'll respect what you want to do because you've been nothing but good to us. I ain't gon' lie though. I hope one day you might change your mind about us but I won't push it."

"You truly are a good woman." I held Lala and kissed her on the forehead. She was nothing like Dior, who was completely complicated but that's who I wanted. I only hoped that it didn't turn out to be the worst decision of my life.

Dior

The Fame

* ⭑ ★ ⭑ *

"I'm not doing this shit!"

"Dior, they've already paid you for it."

"Tell them to sue me. Or better yet, baby, refund them their money." Lorenzo just gave me that look. I was used to it by now so I simply laughed it off.

"It doesn't work like that."

"Abby, what part of I'm not doing that shit don't you get." I watched as she started fidgeting in her chair, something Abby did when I was irritating her, which was often. I knew she thought I was a nightmare as a client but Lorenzo was paying her out the ass so she dealt with it.

"Lorenzo, will you please speak to her. I have some phone calls to make."

"I'm still not doing it," I laughed as Abby walked out the room.

"Why do you like fuckin' wit' her?"

"Because she takes herself way too seriously."

"She should with the amount of money she's making off me."

"So she needs to shut her mouth and do what I tell her to do."

"Dior, you're the one who told her you wanted the co-host job for the new music video show. She had to bust her ass to get the network to even consider you. But you said that's what you wanted so she made it happen. Now the contract has been signed, they cut a check and you want to back out!"

"Nobody told me I would have to be on set at five o'clock in the morning."

"It's only three times a week."

"I don't give a damn if it was once a month, I'm just gettin' in the bed at five o'clock. I don't need that video bullshit anymore anyway now that I just got my reality show deal. I was only doing it so people would have something else to talk to me about besides Sway. That shit happened months ago but every interview I do that's the main topic. I'm over it and I'm over doing that video show. Baby, if they want their money back just give it to them."

"Dior, that's not the point. You don't conduct

business like that. Abby works for a highly reputable firm. It makes her look unprofessional and it makes you look bad too. The contract is only for three months. A driver will pick you up every morning. Just do the show. It's gon' be a minute before the reality show starts airing so this will be a good look for you in the interim."

"Fine, I'll do it. These three months can't be over quick enough though."

"That's my girl. Now come give me a kiss."

"You know I can't resist you." It was true I couldn't resist Lorenzo. I never got tired of feeling his lips against mine. I was ready to fuck him right here in our living room even though Abby was only a room away. That was the effect he had on me.

"I have to go handle some business, but I'll be back."

"You always gotta go handle business."

"If you want me to be able to keep paying for things like a publicist and this fancy ass condo I bought you then I gotta work."

"Don't forget about the party we have to go to tonight."

"How can I forget, it's an everyday thing for you. Don't you get tired of partying every night?"

"Nope, it's part of my job. It keeps me relevant. I dress up. I go to parties. That's what I get paid to do. Why are you looking at me like that?" Lorenzo was leaning against a chair and I was standing between his legs and he was giving me the craziest stare.

"I'm looking at you thinking to myself that never in my wildest dream did I think I would fall for your type."

"Is my type really that bad?"

"Yes, but I love you so it doesn't matter."

"I love you more. I really do. I can't imagine not being with you. When I think how you saved me from that Sway situation."

"I didn't save you."

"Yes you did. I was a prisoner in my own apartment but like you promised you hired the best people to spin this ordeal in my favor. And instead of me coming across as some pathetic chick that got beat up by her boyfriend they made me into this woman everybody wanted to cheer for. How they managed that, I have no idea but appearing on that Diane Sawyer special certainly helped."

"I still wish you didn't accept that settlement deal with Sway. It's not like you needed the money."

"I wanted it to go away. Going to court, having this shit dragged out...I would've never gotten out of Sway's shadow, I'm still not. But it's better than what it would've been. And it's not like he got totally off. Yeah, he pleaded guilty to a lesser charge but he's on probation and knowing Sway he'll fuck that up."

"You shoulda let me fuck him up and we wouldn't even be having this conversation."

"I need you. I can't take any chances of something happening to you, especially over Sway's dumbass. I want him to be so yesterday's news. But what tripped me out was after all that shit his label still put out that video we shot together. They actually thought it would help him sell records and the crazy part was that they were right. But I can't complain it helped me too."

"And this is the industry you want to be in so badly. I don't understand why."

"That's because you're normal, baby. Only crazy people like me and Sway understand. But that's why I love you."

"And I love you."

"You better." I smiled and nuzzled my nose against his.

"Let me get outta here."

"Yeah, let me let you go because I don't want you calling talking about you're not going to make it back in time for the party."

"I'll be here. Now go make nice with Abby."

"Yes, baby, anything for you."

"I'll see you tonight." I already felt sad and Lorenzo had only left my sight a few minutes ago but what made me keep smiling was I knew he would be back.

"I hear all is a go," Abby said in that fake voice and smile she was famous for.

"You know I can never let Lorenzo down, so

yes it's a go."

"Smart decision. I know we don't see eye-to-eye on a lot of things, Dior, but I want this to work. I've been very successful with making you a star virtually overnight. The potential is endless. You're lucky. For some reason people are intrigued by you. Don't blow it."

"Abby, you can go now. I have something important to do. There's this party tonight and I have to find something to wear. You know your way out."

"This is the last stop," I told my driver when we pulled up to the YSL store on 855 Madison Avenue. While I waited for him to open my door, my phone was ringing and it was my baby calling.

"Hey you."

"Don't be mad but I can't make it tonight."

"You promised."

"Dior, I didn't promise."

"You promised in my mind."

"Stop it. What I'm taking care of is taking longer than I thought it would."

"I hate going to parties without you."

"You'll be fine."

"Being with you keeps me safe."

"Dior, go to the party. Call Courtney. She'll be glad to go with you.

"You'll be home tonight though, right?"

"Don't I always come home to you?"

"Yes, I'll see you later tonight."

"Ok, have fun." When I hung up with Lorenzo I called Courtney.

"Hey Courtney."

"Dior! How are you?"

"I'm in a bind actually."

"What is it?"

"I have to go to this party tonight and Lorenzo can't come. I don't want to go by myself. Will you go with me?"

"Of course!"

"Awesome. I'll be downstairs at like ten."

"See you then."

I leaned back in the car and looked down at my hand, playing with the ring Lorenzo had given me on my birthday. I remembered how excited I was when he gave it to me and I asked him, was it an engagement ring. He laughed and told me no, it was a ring that promised that if I stayed out of trouble we would get engaged. So I had been on my best behavior ever since. But tonight for the first time since I got back on the scene after Sway, I was going out without him and I was petrified.

"You can take me home. I'm done shopping for the day," I informed the driver as I held on tightly to my ring as if it had some sort of magical power that would get me through anything.

"Dior, turn this way! Over here, Dior! No this way, Dior!" That's all I heard as I walked the red carpet into the party. The photographers stayed calling my name and I made sure not to give them a fashion fail with my black mini-cutout Roberto Cavalli dress.

"They love you!" Courtney gushed when we finally made it into the party.

"They do, don't they," I smiled.

"Dior, your table is over here," a guy dressed in a black suit said escorting me to the back of the venue. "Your waitress will be bringing over your bottles of champagne shortly."

"Thanks."

"Your life is unbelievable. All people do is cater to you."

"Yeah, they do, don't they, except for the one person I need the most."

"Dior, I'm sure if he could Lorenzo would be here. He loves you so much. I've seen it with my own eyes."

"I guess. If it wasn't for him none of this would be happening for me. It's amazing what money can do, you know."

"But if you didn't have that 'it' factor, all the money in the world couldn't buy you fame. People love you." I wanted to believe that what Courtney said was true but there was this part of me that always felt that people would discover that I wasn't good enough. I had absolutely no talent. But I did have a gift that had taken me very far and it was called determination.

"Courtney, you're right people do love me and we're going to celebrate that. I know you don't drink, but you're going to have some champagne tonight."

"I guess I could have one glass." That one glass turned into a champagne campaign for us. The bottles didn't stop popping all night. With Lorenzo not being here I had nobody to tell me enough and I certainly wasn't going to tell myself. Before long I was dancing on the table and having a blast.

"Come on, Courtney, let's go to the dance floor," I cheered as we both struggled to keep our composure. I was about to fall down when I felt somebody catch me. I was so drunk all I did was laugh until I saw it was Sway.

"Let me go." I was drunk but I knew I didn't want Sway's hands on me.

"I was only trying to help. Come sit down before you hurt yourself." I held onto Sway until we got to his table. "Who are you here with?"

"Courtney. Where did she go?"

"I think I see her over there dancing with some guy."

"We both have had too much to drink."

"You never did know how to put down the champagne. But I think I have something that can balance you out." It was easy for me to figure out what Sway meant. I hadn't really done any drugs since Lorenzo and I started living together but Sway knew me so well and he always gave me what I thought I needed.

"Give it to me." Sway put some lines on the table and I sniffed them up so quickly that it took me a moment to know something was different. "This isn't coke, what is this?"

"I've upgraded, it's heroin. You 'bout to have the best high of your life."

"I need to go home." I instantly regretted sitting down with Sway. But it's like crazy people are drawn to other crazy people.

"That's cool but I'll put the rest in your purse. You can thank me later for it 'cause trust me; you'll be wantin' some more."

I grabbed my purse from Sway and went looking for the exit. On my way out I found Courtney dancing with some guy who was groping all over her. "Let's go!" It was time for both of us to go home.

When we got to Courtney's place I had the driver

take her upstairs to make sure she got inside safely. While I was waiting for him to come down I reached in my purse to get a piece of gum and saw the heroin Sway had put in there. He was right. It had given me the best high ever. The feeling of euphoria was making me want to make love to myself so I couldn't wait to get home so Lorenzo could do it for me.

When I finally got home, Lorenzo was in the living room watching television. I started taking off my clothes at the front door ready for him to make love to me.

"How was the party?" he asked flipping the channels.

"It would've been better if you were there but now I'm home so you can make it up to me." I sat my naked body on Lorenzo's lap and began tugging at his boxer shorts.

"Look at me," he said grabbing my face.

"Baby, if you want a kiss all you have to do is ask, you don't have to grab my face," I giggled.

"Are you high?"

"Huh?"

"Don't huh me. Are you fuckin' high?"

"No! I just had some champagne," I lied turning my face away. Lorenzo yanked it back towards his direction.

"What the fuck are you high on 'cause it ain't champagne." Lorenzo pushed me off of him and picked my purse up from the floor.

"What are you doing!" I yelled out as I tried to get my purse from him. He pushed me away and dumped the belongings inside my purse on the table. He saw the small container and opened it. He put it up to his nose and his face frowned up.

"You been snorting heroin! Are you fuckin' crazy!" he screamed throwing the container against the wall.

"I didn't do that much. I thought it was coke."

"I should've known you were a drug addict. That's why you would never free yourself from Sway—you're a junkie. You were probably gettin' high together."

"I'm not a junkie!"

"When you runnin' 'round wit' heroin in your purse, you a fuckin' junkie!"

"Sway put that in my purse, not me." I couldn't believe I just said that but I was so angry trying to defend myself that it slipped out. From the disgust on Lorenzo's face the damage was done.

"You were with Sway tonight?"

"No but we were both at the party."

"So how did he put heroin in your purse?"

"I was tipsy and he helped me sit down. I thought he was giving me some coke but after I snorted it he told me it was heroin. Then he put the rest in my purse before I left to come home to you."

"You think coming home to me makes it ok that you took heroin from the same man that beat the shit out of you. What the fuck is wrong wit' you?"

"You were supposed to be with me tonight. If you had been there none of this would've happened."

"Now it's my fault you a junkie."

"Would you stop saying that! I'm not a junkie!"

"I know a junkie when I see one. Look at you!" Lorenzo pulled me to a mirror near the fireplace and held me in front of it. "Look at your eyes, that's the face of a junkie. I know a junkie when I see one 'cause my own fuckin' mother was a junkie."

"No your mother is schizophrenia! That's why you won't make a baby with me, remember!"

"Why would I want a druggie whore to carry my baby? So you can destroy it the way you've destroyed yourself."

"I hate you! I hate you so fuckin' much!"

"The feeling is mutual," Lorenzo said, before going into our bedroom. I so badly wanted to pick up something and throw it but knew it wouldn't make my anger go away. A few minutes later Lorenzo came out and he was dressed.

"Where are you going?"

"I'm gettin' the fuck outta here."

"Well fuck you then! Just go! I don't need you anyway!" The last thing I remembered was the door slamming before I passed out and went to sleep.

Lorenzo

Love The Way You Lie

★⁎✬⁎★⁎

I woke up with Lala lying beside me in bed but Dior was the one on my mind. Dior made me so angry last night and when I left her, Lala was the perfect escape. She let me come over without asking me any questions. And while I had sex with her for a brief moment I was able to put Dior and her craziness out of my head. But I woke up with her heavy on mind. My phone was ringing and it was Dior. I debated whether to answer it. I looked over at Lala who was asleep so I went into the hallway and took the call.

"What is it?"

"Baby, I'm sorry. Where are you?"

"At a friend's."

"Please come home. Baby, I'm so sorry. It was being high that made me say those things."

"That's the problem right there. Dior, I can't be with a woman that does drugs. I know firsthand what drugs do to people."

"I'll stop. I'll do whatever you want just please come home." I let out a long sigh. "Please. I won't be able to stop without you."

"Things would have to change, Dior. All that partying shit you do keep you with a fucked up crowd of people."

"But when we're together you make sure I don't get caught up with all that."

"I have shit I need to handle sometimes and I can't be there to hold your hand all the time like you a baby."

"Then I won't go to these parties when you can't be there with me. Lorenzo, baby, please, please come home, please. I'm begging you."

"Dior, don't cry. I'll be home."

"When?"

"I'm coming now."

"You promise."

"Yes, I promise."

"I love you."

"I love you too. I'll be home shortly." When I walked back in the bedroom Lala was standing by the door.

"Why do you love her? She doesn't deserve you, Lorenzo."

"Lala, you shouldn't have been listening to our conversation."

"It doesn't change the fact that I heard it. She's a famewhore, Lorenzo. You don't need a woman like that."

"I respect your opinion but don't ever speak about Dior like that in front of me again."

"Remarkable, that woman can walk all over you and I'm forbidden to say anything negative about her but I'm always here for you but you choose her over me every time."

"Lala, when it comes to you and Dior it's never a choice because she's always first. I never pretended otherwise with you. Yes, I care about you but my relationship with Dior isn't something you need to try and understand."

"I hope you get everything you deserve fuckin' around with her."

"What the hell you mean by that?"

"Nothing, nothing at all. I'ma go make some breakfast for Tania. I'll see you later."

When I got home Dior was in the bed asleep. I went and took a shower then got under the covers with her. She looked so peaceful. But I couldn't resist kissing her neck and soon I had her nipples in my mouth. "Baby, you're home," she whispered coming out of her sleep.

"I told you I would be."

"Please don't ever leave me again."

"I won't. I love this pussy too much."

"And it loves you back." When I slid inside Dior I knew she was right. It always felt like the first time when we made love. "Baby, you feel so good. I don't ever want another man inside of me, only you."

"Are you sure?"

"Positive, just don't leave me." The more Dior talked the harder my dick got. It was like her voice was seducing me.

"I'll never leave you again. I promise you that," I moaned as I continued twisting her insides out. She was so wet. I was drowning inside of her.

"Lorenzo."

"What is it?" Dior was gazing into my eyes as if she was staring into my soul.

"Please let me have your baby. I'll be everything you want me to be."

"Can you give up that life?"

"If it means having a part of you—yes."

"Ok, we'll have a baby."

"I love you so much," Dior called out, spreading her legs even wider apart as if she hoped I would drop a seed in her right now.

For the rest of the day and night Dior and I stayed in the bed. All we did was make love, watch

TV, talk and eat. I think it was the most fun we ever had. When we woke up the next morning I decided it was time I opened myself all the way up to her.

"You still haven't told me where we're going."

"We're going to visit my mother at the mental facility she's at."

"I know you're worried. But because your mother is ill doesn't mean our baby will have the same mental illness."

"You're right and if you're willing to take that chance then so am I."

"But I'm glad you're taking me to see your mother. I want to know and understand everything that makes you feel the way you do."

"My mother walked out on us when I was seven years old. My father had to raise me by himself. After my mother left it's like he swore off having any sort of meaningful relationship with a woman."

"Do you know why your mother left?"

"My father said it was because she was tired of being poor and no longer wanted the responsibility of raising a child."

"But your father was there, wasn't he helping your mother raise you?"

"All he did was work. But they were bullshit jobs that barely paid the bills. By the time he got home he would sleep for a couple hours and then go to his next job."

"Is that why you work so hard now because you don't want to be poor like your father?"

"Damn right. My dad busted his ass working every single day only to be shitted on when he got sick because he had no medical insurance. Nobody cared. They let him die with no dignity."

"Baby, I'm sorry."

"Don't be. Watching what happened to my father let me understand that in this fucked up world the only thing that separates people is what's in their pocket. And my dad found that out the hard way. Before he died he made it clear to me to do whatever I had to do to make sure my pockets were never low."

"My mother was just the opposite. She acted like wanting money was a crime. She had me by a married man that wouldn't give her a dime for my care. It was like she blamed me for losing him. It was like after their relationship ended she totally let herself go—she looked horrible. I started thinking she did it on purpose so no man would want her. When I would talk about my dreams and wanting something better out of life she would say my daddy didn't want me and I would never amount to nothing. As soon as I turned eighteen I left that miserable hellhole and never looked back."

"Do you talk to your mother at all?"

"Every blue moon but I think she was glad

when I left. I was nothing but a constant reminder that her so called great love didn't want her."

"I want you," I said lifting up Dior's hand and kissing it, "that's all that matters."

"You're right. Being with you is all I need. I could ride in this car with you forever and be perfectly content."

"Well, our riding has come to an end for the time being, because we have arrived."

"Wow, this place is beautiful. It looks more like a resort than a mental facility."

"It's too bad my mother doesn't know it." I took Dior's hand and we went to my mother's room. When we got there she was sitting by the same window looking outside.

"What a beautiful view she has."

"That was the reason I picked this room. It has one of the best views in the entire facility. Every time I come she's always looking out that window."

"You may think your mother isn't aware of things but there's a reason she's always looking out that window."

"Hey mom, I want you to meet, Dior. She's the woman that I'm going to marry, be the mother of my child and spend the rest of my life with."

"Are you serious?"

"I wouldn't have said it if I wasn't."

"Does this mean my promise ring is now an engagement ring?"

"No, we're gonna pick out a new ring that represents a new beginning for us. You hear that, mom. You're gonna gain a daughter-in-law and grandchild, hopefully all within the next year."

I bent down and held my mother's hands. I didn't know if it was wishful thinking or really true but I swore I felt her squeeze my hand.

"I know you don't know me, but I really do love your son. Day by day he's saving me from myself. And I'm going to do everything I can to make him the happiest man in the world."

"Come here," I reached out my hand and pulled Dior close. "You've already made me the happiest man in the world."

"How's that, when I've been doing nothing but screwing up."

"You made me fall in love and I thank you for that."

"Baby, you sure I can't come with you to your office. You never let me go with you when you work."

"One thing at a time. I'll only be gone for a few hours and then we're gonna go out and celebrate our engagement so wear something extremely obscene tonight."

"You're so silly but aren't all my clothes

obscene?"

"Then put on something extra obscene. Bye sexy, I'll see you later." Dior blew me a kiss and I hated that I had to leave her but I needed to handle this meeting at my office which I didn't think would take long.

When I was coming out the Holland Tunnel I saw that Alexus was calling but when I answered she either hung up or the call dropped. I called her back but it went straight to voicemail. I decided to wait until I got to my office to call her again. When I pulled up to the parking lot everyone seemed to already be there so I wasted no time getting upstairs. When the elevator doors opened up everybody was huddled as if in crisis mode.

"What's all this about?" Each of them looked up at me simultaneously with the same bleak look in their eyes. "Yo, why is everybody so quiet? We got another situation where it ain't cool to talk in here?"

"Everything is cool in here, we triple checked this mutherfucker," Brice assured me.

"Then why you all looking like somebody died?"

"We think something might've happened to Alexus."

"That can't be she just called me."

"You spoke to her?"

"No, I got a call from her but when I answered we got disconnected."

"Did you try to call her back?"

"Yeah and it went straight to voicemail. Why do you think something foul happened?"

"Because when we went to her crib it had been ransacked. There was shit everywhere."

"I knew I shoulda murked that bitch."

"Yo, Lorenzo, what are you talkin' 'bout? Alexus is fam."

"I'm telling you ain't nothin' happened to her. I always felt like she had something to do with that kidnapping shit."

"We checked her out and she came back clean. I told you there were some Dominican dudes behind it but we lost our trace on them."

"Them mutherfuckers were able to get too close without having some inside help."

"Darnell, was their inside help. I'm telling you, Alexus is clean. Them Dominican niggas came back to get her ass."

"Why? They got the fuckin' money. They didn't need to come back for Alexus. That sheisty bitch was in on that shit from the jump! She done took her cut and broke the fuck out. But that's a'right we gon' find her ass. It may take a year or two but she can't hide forever.

"So if she in on it, why did she call you?"

"Brice, that's all game. She been tryna plan

her departure. She want us to believe some fucked up shit happened to her so we be looking for a dead body and not a live one. Did you call her mother's crib in North Carolina?"

"Yes," he nodded.

"And what did she say?"

"The number was disconnected."

"All of us fucked up big time wit' this bullshit." I was angry as hell. I was so busy chasing behind Dior and attending bullshit parties with her that I let my business slip. Now that trifling ass Alexus had bounced with her cut of the money. But just like Darnell she would pay the consequences for her betrayal.

Dior

I Hate That I Love You

"I guess you forgot that you told me you would be here three hours ago," was how I greeted Lorenzo when he finally came home.

"Today was a fucked up day," he countered tossing his keys on the table.

"What happened?"

"Just bullshit. I got so many bullshit people in my life, I'm sick of all of them."

"Why don't you fire them and hire some new people?"

"If it was only that easy."

"What exactly do you do? I mean you say that you have your hands in a lot of different things but what sort of things?"

"What do you think?"

"I know you do some things with Phenomenon."

"And what else?"

"Stop with the riddles, Lorenzo, can't you just answer the question."

"I make money. That's what I do and I make a fuckin' lot of it. And because I make so much fuckin' money I'm constantly dealing wit' bullshit. Real bullshit, not that dumb shit you get yourself involved in."

"Why are you bringing me in this?"

"Because if I wasn't so busy holding your hand every damn day I would've been more focused on my business and would've squashed this shit a long time ago before it grew some legs."

"I'm sorry I fucked things up for you." I tried to hold them back but the tears just started flowing.

"Damn Dior, can you stop being so dramatic all the fuckin' time. What's up with the tears!"

"Do you think I want to cry right now! I don't understand you. Earlier today you were telling your mother I was going to be your wife and the mother of your child now you're telling me I'm fuckin' up your life. I'm trying so hard for you but I can't get it right. It's like you hate that you love me."

"Don't put words in my mouth."

"That's how you act."

"Dior, I'm not in the mood to pacify you right

now."

"That's fine. I guess we won't be going out to celebrate our engagement after all, so I'm going to bed."

Lorenzo's cold demeanor towards me put a chill through my body. So after throwing off my clothes to take a shower my feet welcomed the heated floors in the bathroom. It was a warmth that Lorenzo seemed to be able to turn on and off at his convenience. I had never tried so hard to please one man who always made me feel like I would never measure up. I turned off all the lights in the bathroom because I didn't even want to look at myself anymore. The one person who I needed to love me instead constantly rejected me.

I stayed in the hot shower so long by the time I got out when I hit the bed my eyes closed shut. When I felt warm, strong hands rubbing up my body at first I thought I was dreaming but then a voice said, "Don't ever think I don't love you because I do." His soft lips kissed my earlobes and I instantly got wet. I turned over and my body was his without him even asking. He lifted me up so I would be on top. At first I screamed out as I shifted my hips to take all of him inside of me. But as my back arched and his hands and tongue played with my nipples I kept riding Lorenzo harder welcoming the pain. We both wanted more and we gave it to each other because soon our pleasures hit the ultimate high as we climaxed together. That night Lorenzo fell asleep inside me and never moved. It seemed we became one and for the first time I truly believed he did love me.

"Baby, what's that noise?" I asked not wanting to wake up but unable to ignore the loud banging.

"I think somebody's at the door."

"Oh shit. That's probably Abby. I forgot we're supposed to meet this morning. Can you go get it, baby? I need a few more minutes before I have to go deal with her."

"No problem." When Lorenzo got up to put on his boxer shorts I wanted to pull him back in bed with me because I was getting wet all over again. Instead I closed my eyes so I could try to get five more minutes of sleep. But loud commotion was coming from the living room and I had to see what the hell was going on. I put on my bathrobe and when I walked out there were more than a dozen law enforcement officers. I couldn't tell if it was the DEA, The Feds or what, all I saw was black clothes, badges and guns.

"Lorenzo Taylor, you're under arrest for money laundering, running a continuing criminal enterprise, murder of Darnell Hobbs...," after the word murder I couldn't hear anything after that. My mind began drifting to a million different places all the while my eyes remained locked with Lorenzo's. I was waiting for him to tell me what I was supposed to do but he never said a word. I couldn't take it anymore.

"Baby, what am I supposed to do?"

"It'll be okay. I'll call you," he said calmly as if he wasn't about to go to jail. They let him put on some clothes and I stood there watching feeling helpless. As they were taking him out some woman stopped him in his tracks.

"Before you left, I wanted you to see the face of the woman responsible for bringing you down."

"Why would you do this, Lala?"

"Alexus told me everything. You murdered the father of my child and then took me to bed and played daddy to his daughter. You're a cold hearted bastard and I can't wait for you to spend the rest of your life behind bars."

"Lorenzo, what is she talking about? Lorenzo, answer me," but he never looked in my direction as they escorted him out in handcuffs.

"Don't shed a tear for him, Dior."

"Excuse me? I don't even know you so don't tell me what I should or shouldn't do."

"Why would you want to cry over a man that was cheating on you the entire time you all were together?"

"You're a liar!"

"The other night when he didn't come home because he found out you were high on drugs, he was with me. He told me how pathetic you are and the only reason he stayed with you was because he felt sorry for you. He bought a big beautiful home for me and my daughter because he wanted us to be a family. You were nothing more than a charity case to him. So don't waste your tears on that sonofabitch, he'll be spending the rest of his life behind bars anyway."

When she left and the door closed, I completely lost it. I felt sick like I wanted to die. I ran to the bathroom and threw up. I continued to vomit until all I was coughing up was air. I leaned over the side of the toilet and just cried. I didn't realize I had so many tears in me. It felt like that moment was the end of my life.

Lorenzo

Who Will Survive

★★★★★

"Dior, I can't describe how good it feels to see your face. I've missed you, baby."

"I've missed you too. But I hate seeing you in a place like this. You don't belong in jail."

"And I won't be for long. I have the best attorney's working to get me out. I'm not worried about me I'm concerned about you. How are you holding up?"

"Not good. I don't have anybody to talk to. I mean Courtney she listens and she tries to be there for me but it's so hard."

"Baby, please don't start crying. We're gonna

get through this together."

"Do you love me, Lorenzo?"

"Of course, why would you even ask me that?"

"Then why, why were you seeing her?"

"Seeing who, Lala?"

"Yes."

"Dior, that was before you. When we got serious, I cut it off. Tania is my Goddaughter so I did take care of them but after we became serious I cut it off with her—I promise you."

"What about that night you didn't come home after we got into that huge argument, did you stay with her?"

"Yes, I stayed at her house."

"Did you have sex with her?" I looked away because it was killing me that I was literally watching myself break Dior's heart.

"Why are you doing this, Dior? I love you, I've always loved you. I swear on everything, you are the only woman besides my mother that I've ever loved. You have my heart. That's all that matters."

"Did you have sex with her that night, Lorenzo?"

"Yes, but it was a mistake. I was pissed at you because of that whole situation with Sway but it meant nothing. I came back home to you."

"Yeah, because you felt sorry for me. You think I'm pathetic."

"What are you talkin' about? I don't feel sorry

for you. I came back home because I love you and I wanted to be with you. I still do."

"I want to believe you but you have this whole life that you kept from me. You didn't even trust me enough to tell me what was going on. And now you're in jail because some woman you were having sex with turned on you. Everybody seems to know everything but me."

"Dior, it's not like that. You know I can't go into details but trust it's me and you. When I get out we will be together. We will have that wedding and make that baby like we said we would—believe that. I know my time is about to be up but I'ma call you tomorrow."

"Okay."

"Dior, be strong. I love you don't ever doubt that."

"I love you too, baby."

That night I dreamed about getting out and being with Dior again. I promised myself that I would never take her for granted or make her feel that my love for her wasn't real. Going through this bullshit made me realize what was truly important. I had so much and was this close to losing it all because of bad decisions. But I had no doubt I would beat the case and be back home to Dior.

The next day, the first opportunity I got I

called Dior. I told her I would and I knew she was already feeling insecure about our relationship. I didn't want to put anymore doubt in her head.

"Hi, Lorenzo, I was hoping you would call."

"Who is this?" the woman's voice sounded so muzzled I couldn't recognize it.

"Courtney."

"Oh hey, Courtney. Can I speak to Dior?"

"Dior isn't here."

"She stepped out, when will she be back?"

"She's not coming back. Dior died last night."

"What did you just say?"

"Dior died of a drug overdose last night. When I came over early this morning, I found her body." There was a long pause and I could hear Courtney crying. "I'm sorry. I've been trying to hold it together. I've been crying off and on for hours and I thought I was done. But telling you..." her voice trailed off and I heard more sobbing. While she was crying it was hard for me to process what I was hearing. I had just seen Dior's beautiful face yesterday and now she was gone. What Courtney was saying seemed surreal to me. "Lorenzo, are you still there?"

"Yes." Was the only word I was able to say.

"I'm so sorry you had to find out like this. I know you loved her and so did I. She was everything I wanted to be. But now I don't want this anymore. I'm going back to school because I want a regular life. Fame killed her, Lorenzo. Without you being here she couldn't handle it."

I couldn't listen anymore to what Courtney was saying. My mind was blown and my heart felt like it stopped beating and I had died. I fell to the floor and just cried. I remembered as a child, when my mother left me I'd promised myself, I would never cry over another woman again. I guess that's why they tell you, never say never because I knew for the rest of my life I would shed many more tears over losing Dior.

The End

Read The Entire Bitch Series in This Order

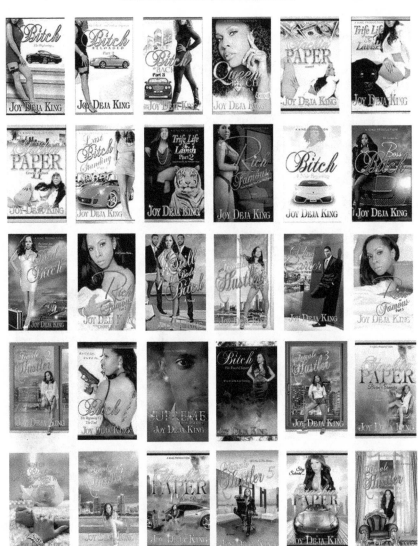

Coming Soon

A KING PRODUCTION

All I See Is The Money...

Female Hustler 7

A Novel

JOY DEJA KING

A KING PRODUCTION

Stackin' PAPER

a novel

JOY DEJA KING

Chapter One
A Killer Is Born

Philly, 1993

"Please, Daquan, don't hit me again!" the young mother screamed, covering her face in defense mode. She hurriedly pushed herself away from her predator, sliding her body on the cold hardwood floor.

"Bitch, get yo' ass back over here!" he barked, grabbing her matted black hair and dragging her into the kitchen. He reached for the hot skillet from the top of the oven, and you could hear the oil popping underneath the fried chicken his wife had been cooking right before he came home. "Didn't I tell you to have my food ready on the table when I came home?"

"I... I... I was almost finished, but you came home early," Teresa stuttered, "Ouch!" she yelled as her neck damn near snapped when Daquan gripped her hair even tighter.

"I don't want to hear your fuckin' excuses. That's what yo' problem is. You so damn hard headed and neva want to listen. But like they say, a hard head make fo' a soft ass. You gon' learn to listen to me."

"Please, please, Daquan, don't do this! Let me finish frying your chicken and I'll never do this again. Your food will be ready and on the table everyday on time. I promise!"

"I'm tired of hearing your damn excuses."

"Bang!" was all you heard as the hot skillet came crashing down on Teresa's head. The hot oil splashed up in the air, and if Daquan hadn't moved forward and turned his head, his face would've been saturated with the grease.

But Teresa wasn't so lucky, as the burning oil grazed her hands, as they were protecting her face and part of her thigh.

After belting out in pain from the grease, she then noticed blood trickling down from the open gash on the side of her forehead. But it didn't stop there. Daquan then put the skillet down and began kicking Teresa in her ribs and back like she was a diseased infected dog that had just bitten him.

"Yo', Pops, leave moms alone! Why you always got to do this? It ain't never no peace when you come in this house." Genesis stood in the kitchen entrance with his fists clenched and panting like a bull. He had grown sick and tired of watching his father beat his mother down almost every single day. At the age of eleven he had seen his mother receive more ass whippings than hugs or any indication of love.

"Boy, who the fuck you talkin' to? You betta get yo' ass back in your room and stay the hell outta of grown people's business."

"Genesis, listen to your father. I'll be alright. Now go

back to your room," his mother pleaded.

Genesis just stood there unable to move, watching his mother and feeling helpless. The blood was now covering her white nightgown and she was covering her midsection, obviously in pain trying to protect the baby that was growing inside of her. He was in a trance, not knowing what to do to make the madness stop. But he was quickly brought back to reality when he felt his jaw almost crack from the punch his father landed on the side of his face.

"I ain't gon' tell you again. Get yo' ass back in your room! And don't come out until I tell you to! Now go!" Daquan didn't even wait to let his only son go back to his room. He immediately went over to Teresa and picked up where he left off, punishing her body with punches and kicks. He seemed oblivious to the fact that not only was he killing her, but also he was killing his unborn child right before his son's eyes.

A tear streamed down Genesis's face as he tried to reflect on one happy time he had with his dad, but he went blank. There were no happy times. From the first moment he could remember, his dad was a monster.

All Genesis remembered starting from the age of three was the constant beat downs his mother endured for no reason. If his dad's clothes weren't ironed just right, then a blow to the face. If the volume of the television was too loud, then a jab here. And, God forbid, if the small, two-bedroom apartment in the drug-infested building they lived in wasn't spotless, a nuclear bomb would explode in the form of Daquan. But the crazy part was, no matter how clean their apartment was or how good the food was cooked and his clothes being ironed just right, it was never good enough. Daquan would bust in the door, drunk or high, full of anger, ready to take out all his frustration out on his wife. The dead end jobs, being broke, living in the drug infested and violent prone city of Philadelphia had turned the already troubled man into poison to his whole family.

"Daddy, leave my mom alone," Genesis said in a calm, unemotional tone. Daquan kept striking Teresa as if he didn't hear his son. "I'm not gonna to tell you again. Leave my mom alone." This time Daquan heard his son's warning but seemed unfazed.

"I guess that swollen jaw wasn't enough for you. You dying to get that ass beat." Daquan looked down at a now black and blue Teresa who seemed to be about to take her last breath. "You keep yo' ass right here, while I teach our son a lesson." Teresa reached her hand out with the little strength she had left trying to save her son. But she quickly realized it was too late. The sins of the parents had now falling upon their child.

"Get away from my mother. I want you to leave and don't ever come back."

Daquan was so caught up in the lashing he had been putting on his wife that he didn't even notice Genesis retrieving the gun he left on the kitchen counter until he had it raised and pointed in his direction. "Lil' fuck, you un lost yo' damn mind! You gon' make me beat you with the tip of my gun."

Daquan reached his hand out to grab the gun out of Genesis's hand, and when he moved his leg forward, it would be the last step he'd ever take in his life. The single shot fired ripped through Daquan's heart and he collapsed on the kitchen floor, dying instantly.

Genesis was frozen and his mother began crying hysterically.

"Oh dear God!" Teresa moaned, trying to gasp for air. "Oh, Genesis baby, what have you done?" She stared at Daquan, who laid face up with his eyes wide open in shock. He died not believing until it was too late that his own son would be the one to take him out this world.

It wasn't until they heard the pounding on the front door that Genesis snapped back to the severity of the situation at hand.

"Is everything alright in there?" they heard the older lady from across the hall ask.

Genesis walked to the door still gripping the .380-caliber semi-automatic. He opened the door and said in a serene voice, "No, Ms. Johnson, everything is *not* alright. I just killed my father."

****

Two months later, Teresa cried as she watched her son being taking away to spend a minimum of two years in a juvenile facility in Pemberton, New Jersey.

Although it was obvious by the bruises on both Teresa and Genesis that he acted in self defense, the judge felt that the young boy having to live with the guilt of murdering his own father wasn't punishment enough. He concluded that if Genesis didn't get a hard wake up call, he would be headed on a path of self destruction. He first ordered him to stay at the juvenile facility until he was eighteen. But after pleas from his mother, neighbors and his teacher, who testified that Genesis had the ability to accomplish whatever he wanted in life because of how smart and gifted he was, the judge reduced it to two years, but only if he demonstrated excellent behavior during his time there. Those two years turned into four and four turned into seven. At the age of eighteen when Genesis was finally released he was no longer a young boy, he was now a criminal minded man.

ORDER FORM

Name:

Address:

City/State:

Zip:

QUANTITY	TITLES	PRICE	TOTAL
	Bitch	$15.00	
	Bitch Reloaded	$15.00	
	The Bitch Is Back	$15.00	
	Queen Bitch	$15.00	
	Last Bitch Standing	$15.00	
	Superstar	$15.00	
	Ride Wit' Me	$12.00	
	Ride Wit' Me Part 2	$15.00	
	Stackin' Paper	$15.00	
	Trife Life To Lavish	$15.00	
	Trife Life To Lavish II	$15.00	
	Stackin' Paper II	$15.00	
	Rich or Famous	$15.00	
	Rich or Famous Part 2	$15.00	
	Rich or Famous Part 3	$15.00	
	Bitch A New Beginning	$15.00	
	Mafia Princess Part 1	$15.00	
	Mafia Princess Part 2	$15.00	
	Mafia Princess Part 3	$15.00	
	Mafia Princess Part 4	$15.00	
	Mafia Princess Part 5	$15.00	
	Boss Bitch	$15.00	
	Baller Bitches Vol. 1	$15.00	
	Baller Bitches Vol. 2	$15.00	
	Baller Bitches Vol. 3	$15.00	
	Bad Bitch	$15.00	
	Still The Baddest Bitch	$15.00	
	Power	$15.00	
	Power Part 2	$15.00	
	Drake	$15.00	
	Drake Part 2	$15.00	
	Female Hustler	$15.00	
	Female Hustler Part 2	$15.00	
	Female Hustler Part 3	$15.00	
	Female Hustler Part 4	$15.00	
	Female Hustler Part 5	$15.00	
	Female Hustler Part 6	$15.00	
	Princess Fever "Birthday Bash"	$6.00	
	Nico Carter The Men Of The Bitch Series	$15.00	
	Bitch The Beginning Of The End	$15.00	
	Supreme...Men Of The Bitch Series	$15.00	
	Bitch The Final Chapter	$15.00	
	Stackin' Paper III	$15.00	
	Men Of The Bitch Series And The Women Who Love Them	$15.00	
	Coke Like The 80s	$15.00	
	Baller Bitches The Reunion Vol. 4	$15.00	
	Stackin' Paper IV	$15.00	
	The Legacy	$15.00	
	Lovin' Thy Enemy	$15.00	
	Stackin' Paper V	$15.00	
	The Legacy Part 2	$15.00	
	Assassins - Episode 1	$11.00	
	Assassins - Episode 2	$11.00	
	Assassins - Episode 2	$11.00	
	Bitch Chronicles	$40.00	
	So Hood So Rich	$15.00	
	Stackin' Paper VI	$17.99	

Shipping/Handling (Via Priority Mail) $7.50 1-2 Books, $15.00 3-4 Books add $1.95 for ea. Additional book.
Total: $_____FORMS OF ACCEPTED PAYMENTS: Certified or government issued checks and money Orders, all mail in orders take 5-7 Business days to be delivered

9 781942 217701